A Corpse In The Vale

GL

Cover design by Howard Thomas

A catalogue record of this book is available from the British Library

First Edition: May 2003

ISBN: 1-84375-019-X

To order additional copies of this book and other titles by Howard Thomas please visit: http://www.upso.co.uk/howardthomas.htm

Published by: UPSO Ltd
5 Stirling Road, Castleham Business Park,
St Leonards-on-Sea, East Sussex TN38 9NW United Kingdom
Tel: 01424 853349 Fax: 0870 191 3991
Email: info@upso.co.uk Web: http://www.upso.co.uk

A Corpse In The Vale

By

Howard Thomas

UPSO

Chapter One

The security light above the outside entrance door of the Compton Arms, flickered briefly to full illumination capacity and instantly died. This rude awakening disturbed the pub's cat, who until then had been sound asleep, stretched out across the top of a beer barrel. As the door opened, the cat scuttled from its 'midnight sabbatical' away into the night. The slight noise left by its departure was the result of the empty container scraping the tarmac and its subsequent impact against the building.

A continental voice in broken English was clearly audible to the figure who was crouched beside the Toyota MR6 sports car in the darkness of the car park.

"It ees only the damn cat Senor Mitchell. If you 'ang on 'uno momento' I vill get a torch pronto."

Mr. Herbert Mitchell was already a tired man. The business with this Spanish pub manager Senor Stephano had taken far longer than he'd anticipated. Being the senior partner in the accountancy firm of Mitchell and Roberts, the responsibility of visiting new clients to the practice fell to him. Usually, he looked forward to such meetings. It made a pleasant change from poring over such things as the complexities of Capital Gains Tax, VAT, Corporate Tax and the like. Frustration however, crept in when you had to deal with a 'two-bit' foreigner and a pub that barely turned-over £80,000 a year.

Such an operation should in fairness have taken no longer than an hour of his time but as soon as he'd met Mr Edwardo Stephano, he knew from past experience that such a man would be 'pumping' him for information. True to his thoughts – he'd been at the Compton Arms for nearly three hours but because of the hospitality of Maria, the landlord's charming wife, he had been most reluctant to leave. Had it just have been the peasant husband, he'd have made his excuses earlier but it was difficult to ignore the senorita's Latin eyes!

Of course, running a pub had meant that getting the two of them together for more than ten minutes at a time had proved impossible during licensing hours so that the real business talk had only been achieved since closing time.

Herbert reflected regretfully that during that period he'd been obliged to discuss accountancy methods with the husband alone, as Mrs Stephano presumably had more important things to see to. Either that or Edwardo had spoken to her about her blatant flirting. He smiled as he remembered the suggestive look in her eyes as she'd reached across him to pour the tea on introduction. They were sat side by side on the sofa in the cosy upstairs lounge and he recalled again the long curve of her leg, the eau-de-cologne, and the warmth of her touch as her hand brushed across his thigh as she withdrew, having gently placed the cup and saucer in his outstretched palm.

It was a pity she was not here now as he stood waiting to say his goodbyes.

Senor Stephano made as if to go back into the pub to fetch a flashlight but Herbert cut him short.

"No really," he said "it will not be necessary. I can find my own way to the car. Its not as if I've parked half a mile away is it?"

"You are sure Mr Mitchell sir?" came the flustered Spaniard's reply. "It will only take a few moments. I have a torch in zee cellar!"

Herbert ran his fingers across his brow. The man was tiresome and he could feel a mental headache coming along.

"No," he said, surprised at the sharpness of his voice. "Its late but the books ...." he gestured with his hands. "The books that need auditing" he repeated.

The little man looked confused for a second.

"Ah ye-s of course zee books – that was what you came for. Yes?"

He reached back inside for the two red accounting books resting by the telephone on the hallway table.

"I'll let you have them back inside the week" Herbert said as he tucked them under his arm. "Please give my regards to Mrs Stephano and thank her for the tea. I'll be in touch."

"Thank you Mr Mitchell sir. Keep to the right-hand side of the wall as you approach zee car park. Zee barrels are on the left you see!"

"I will. Goodnight Mr Stephano."

Herbert gingerly began to walk towards his car being careful to stay close to the wall as advised. He took deep breaths along the way. The fresh bracing November air was a pleasant tonic after the stuffiness of the centrally heated lounge which he'd been confined to. Rooms without ventilation seriously affected him and that damn lounge was probably responsible for the now severe pain in his temple. Subconsciously his mind slipped back to when he was a child and his then incessant complaining about the cold and draughts. That had of course been in the Fifties in a terraced house devoid of such things as heating apart from a coal fire in the back room. Didn't call them lounges in those days. Old habits die-hard. He could easily afford central heating now of course but preferred to do without. Funny that! When he was a kid, he'd have loved such luxury – now he couldn't stand it, even though it was commonplace.

Apart from the kicking of an old tin can, which set a cat off in the neighbouring garden, Herbert reached his car without further incident. He unlocked the driver's door and was –reassured to see the interior light beckoning. Nonchalantly he tossed the books into the passenger seat and clambered in behind the wheel. Before closing the door he re-adjusted the light so that it would remain on. Remembering his policy of always having a quick perusal of a new client's books before leaving their premises, he reached over and picked up the first volume. By the limited light available he was forced to lean over towards the passenger side in order to peruse the figures.

"The light in these sports cars is bloody awful," he thought to himself but despite this he flicked over the first page and began to read.

It wasn't quite what he'd expected. The full realisation of what was before him did not have an opportunity to materialise. In short, Herbert Mitchell's migraine was instantly blasted right out of his skull and replaced by another medical term – fear. Fear travels in many disguises but in this case, the trauma was brought on by the sense of cold steel pressed unceremoniously into the back of his neck. The voice that accompanied the intrusion into his privacy was muffled and disguised.

"Don't turn around. Do exactly as I say. Although you can't see it, what you are feeling is the squat nose of a Luger pistol. Now rise very slowly."

Herbert did not need a second reminder. He hadn't reached his mid-forties as a respected accountant without learning when to do as he was ordered.

Qualification had required endless hours of superior's demanding work of a high standard in a short space of time. Besides, he'd never been one to question someone of authority. He'd tried it once when he was a kid of course – didn't every little boy? All he'd received for his questioning of authority then was a belt round the ear. Since then he'd earned his place in society by using his brains. Money came easier that way without the need for physical violence and he intended, if he could, to spend considerable more piles without changing his ideas at this late stage.

Slowly and with what he considered to be dignity, Herbert eased himself upright into the driving seat. The metal followed him up and remained pressed against his neck. He chanced a nervous question.

"What's this all about?"

Again the muffled response. His attacker sounded as if they were talking with effort through a gag. This time Herbert thought he could distinguish a cultured accent but he couldn't place the voice.

"No questions or your *dead.*" The last word was emphasised strongly. "Your windscreen will become the same red colour as the car. Now turn off the interior light, turn on the ignition and drive. When you reach the car park exit – turn right!"

Nervously Herbert did precisely as he was told. It was an absurd paradox that here he was driving on a night made for music, not murder. A romantic might say driving a sports car through a peaceful English village on a starry night must be heaven, especially if one was fortunate enough to be in the company of a beautiful blonde but what did he get? Under different circumstances he could concede such a thought but it was nigh on impossible to equate the car, village and the sky with a piece of forged steel rammed almost through your throat.

"Take the next left" came the voice again. This time it was a voice more like gravel. Herbert wondered whether his assailant might not do a good impressionist act on the 'Opportunity Knocks' TV show. This could not be happening to him. What about his wife and son? Would they ever believe him? Probably not. He was considered by all who knew him to be a staid, reliable and boring accountant. That being the case, he promised that all this would change, should he be fortunate enough to escape this nightmare.

They were travelling at speed now, as they approached the outskirts of Compton village. "Damn it," Herbert thought to himself. "Why was it that this place was always asleep?" Little street lighting – place was a terrific example of what happened after the holocaust. At least if a car came up behind him, he might catch a glimpse in the rear mirror of the figure crouched behind his seat. No such luck!

He swung the car left as ordered. In order to make the turn, he had to brake suddenly thereby locking the rear wheels into a skid.

"That was stupid," said the voice. "Keep your speed at thirty."

For the next mile Herbert concentrated on the driving. His

mind wandered no more. It was all he could do to keep the low-slung vehicle on the single tracked excuse for a country lane. There was no tarmac on this god-forsaken stretch of Worcestershire. The damn carriageway was no more than a dirt track bridleway with the customary raised green strip in the middle. In fact it was narrow enough to be a footpath. He had no idea where they were headed but with the beads of perspiration beginning to trickle down his face – he hoped he was near journey's end.

For Herbert Mitchell who at the moment felt like a fugitive from The Twilight Zone, journey's end was indeed fast approaching but not in the way that he would have wished. It is fair to say that if he had indeed known, some of that hidden boyhood aggression may well have come to the surface. As it was, he continued with his trust in God to obey orders.

"Slow down here and turn right by that white post," the voice gruffed.

The main beam of the Toyota's headlights picked out a weather beaten sign in black calligraphy on a white background 'Peaceful Waters'.

He swung the wheel round to the right through an opened gateway and the car bumped its way along a freshly cindered track, bounded on both sides by corralled, naturally seasoned wooden fencing. Further on, the fencing merged into an avenue of towering firs and the cinders changed to pebble-dashed gravel. The initial effect was to a welcomed visitor – breathtaking. To Herbert however, his fear had increased as the closeness of the destination loomed ahead. The headlights, once confined to the closeness of trees, suddenly fanned out like a searchlight as a small country mansion came into view. Alongside the house were two freshly built garages, one of which was open.

"Drive in!" the voice commanded "and cut the headlights. Keep the engine running."

Those were the penultimate words that Herbert Mitchell heard. As the car coasted to a halt, for a fraction of a second the tension of the gun against his neck was relieved. He opened his mouth with the intention of saying "Now what?" The words could not be uttered as he felt a hand clamping his face and a material smothering his nose and gaping mouth. There was a faint almost sweet smell within the material.

His body told him he should struggle but the smell was not unpleasant. He was tired, exhausted even and his eyelids began to droop heavily. It was all a bad dream, Herbert was telling himself – "I shouldn't have been unfaithful to Joyce. It's retribution. I'll awake in a moment and laugh about it." But Herbert didn't awake, unconsciousness set-in!

The shadowy figure removed the chloroform filled handkerchief, satisfied by the slumped position of the driver that he was well anaesthetised.

The kidnapper moved fast in escaping through the passenger side of the vehicle. A length of hose was quickly attached to the exhaust pipe of the stationary Toyota and run along the outside of the bodywork and in through the driver's side window. The sidelights were cut. A cursory check of the fuel gauge was undertaken by flashlight and the figure, dressed all in black, then moved effortlessly outside. An arm reached up for the overhead garage door and pulled.

A creaking, almost screeching sound, pierced the night-time air as the door clanked down over un-oiled hinges. The car was entombed in a brick vault. Still the engine 'ticked over' .....

Chapter Two

It was at about 2am that the swirling mists, which had congregated above the Cotswold Hills, began to descend over Cheltenham in the south and make their way northwards towards Stratford-on-Avon.

At the same time to the west above the Malvern Hills a similar weather phenomenon was taking place, the outcome of which was a dense fog settling over the Vale of Evesham area by the time dawn arrived at 07.02am.

At 8.12am during the build up of morning traffic on the A435 Cheltenham to Evesham road, an articulated lorry shed its load of rolls of newspaper print at a notorious black spot approaching Compton village. In the opposite direction, an early morning sales representative on his way to Birmingham was helpless as one of the hundredweight rolls careered down the hill smashing the windscreen of his Cortina car like a hammer to a block of ice. The result was early morning chaos as the road was blocked in both directions and with a pea-souper of a fog to deal with, the police had their hands full.

Detective Inspector Dougie Peters was caught in the ensuing traffic jam tailback as he joined it shortly after leaving his home in the picturesque village of Brinton-on-Edge at 8.35am. It was only in the last fortnight that he'd developed the art of precise timing in the journey from his new bungalow to Etherton Police Station. This trip was timed at 23 minutes, enabling him time to park and a cursory 'good morning' to the Desk Sergeant at precisely 9am.

Inspector Peters had been in charge of the Market Town Police HQ for six weeks and already he was restless. The incidences of petty crime within the Worcestershire district area were nothing in comparison with his previous experiences at Main City near London. There, he'd had to deal with murder, rape, arson, stabbings and all kinds of unpleasant crimes and keep one jump ahead of New Scotland Yard. Here, the most serious case he'd been asked to investigate had been a burglary at Hallingdon Hall – the home of the local MP Mrs James Dennington. Even that had been taken out of his hands by West Midlands Crime Officers who had arrested those responsible in Worcester City. Hallingdon Hall was just one of many other such burglaries that the men responsible had admitted to.

It wasn't that he didn't like the area, though the locals were a suspicious lot, it was just that it was difficult to get the adrenalin pumping after twenty years of city policing. He was now nearing 40 years of age, a 'crossroads' in his life and for the life of him he wasn't ready yet to settle permanently to the country cottage with the roses round the door ideal. True, Angela his wife loved it here. The pace of life suited her. She was practising medicine as a doctor at Cheltenham General and the change had been a revelation. Whereas before at Main Hospital she had been continually living on her nerves due to being called in at all hours, now she had a regular working pattern and the change in her had been remarkable. The sullen, sunken eyes were back to their school-girlish best. Always her best feature, these last few weeks had brought back the fresh vitality he'd fallen in love with all those years ago. She slept better to, which in turn had brought benefits to their love life. Before they'd gone months without making love due to their respective careers overlapping and overstretching their physical capabilities. Dougie smiled. Since establishing a home in a fresh air environment rather than a polluted city one, he'd lost count of their loving excursions. What a bloody dilemma! Keep the wife happy and be bored to death with petty crime or risk a divorce and get back to real policing by requesting a transfer.

Peter's wound down the driver's window on the Rover and stuck his head out into the cold damp smog. Visibility was down to 20 yards and he assumed there'd been an accident to create such a jam as this. He reached for the intercom.

"Peters to control – do you read?"

"Go ahead sir," came the crackling response from PC Shone. Dougie mentally visualised the young officer at the other end. He was 21, 6 ft 1 inch and devilishly handsome according to the feedback which he heard from the WPCs. Mentally Dougie thought the lad had the ability to go far but like PC Pitman at Main City, he remembered, the copper needed a kick up the arse every so often. He was too bright for his own good and was forever disappearing when needed for a special task.

"Shone. I appear to be stuck in some sort of road jam on the A435 in all this fog. What's the data?"

"Very serious accident at Compton sir. Lorry and car involved on the hill. Sgt Grainger is co-ordinating at the scene and we've an ambulance and fire engine already there. Both driver's injured; car driver believed critical and is having to be cut-out. We are awaiting a crane to arrive at the scene to lift vehicles and newsprint. Road could be blocked for another two hours."

"Two hours!" thought Dougie to himself "like hell I'll be stuck in this soup-can for two ruddy hours!" He spoke rapidly into the intercom.

"Listen Shone. Contact Sgt Grainger. Let him know I'm in the jam – tell him I want a path cleared for my vehicle immediately and telephone the Chief Constable. Put him in the picture and cancel his appointment with us at 9.30am. He'll understand. Give him my compliments and I'll telephone his office later in the day. Anything else?"

"Well it's not been a quiet night sir. There's been trouble at the nightclub, street fighting, a stabbing and an indecent exposure. We're short of staff too!"

"Do your best lad. I'll be there as soon as I can."

Dougie replaced the receiver and reached into the glove compartment for the flashing beacon. He switched on his hazard warning indicators, placed the magnetic beacon to the roof of the car and inched his way out of the traffic. Driving, carefully within the limitations of the conditions, he moved forward onto the opposite side of the carriageway.

Half a mile further on, his headlights picked out the bulk of the lorry. As he approached he could see it lying on its side like a beached whale, the front cabin hanging precariously over a ditch and crushing the 'drunken sergeant' warning barriers. Losing part of its load had obviously affected the weight distribution thereby upending it on the bend. The front half of the other vehicle, a blue Cortina car, was embedded underneath the lorry's axle and the closer Dougie's car inched, the more resigned he was to the extent of the car driver's predicament. The firemen were working frantically with the cutting gear but from where Dougie was sat, he held out little hope.

Detective Sergeant Les Grainger was in deep discussion with Station Officer Gordon of the Hereford & Worcester Fire Brigade when the Inspector's car horn split the air.

"Who the hell is that idiot?" Gordon asked, his eyes turning towards the stationary headlights at the bottom of the hill.

Les Grainger's eyes followed suit. Through the blanket fog he could just make out the flashing beacon.

"I reckon it's my new boss. Have you met Inspector Peters yet? Ex City job he is – full of pansy ideas like efficiency and punctuality. Trying to bring us into the computer age here. There's a lot of resentment amongst our senior men. I'd best go and see what's narking him! See yer Bob."

"Aye, We'll have one later in the Compton Arms – that's if this bloody stuff ever lifts" came the fire officer's retort. "You going on in his car?"

"Depends. Reckon we might get through on the far side verge. I'll see what his lordship says." He took a pace down the hill – it was a slow one to be sure. Detective Sgt Grainger was a man unused to hurrying things. Life was a marathon to him – not a sprint. True in his younger days, when he'd been a keen raw-faced recruit, life had promised him a lofty ambition – perhaps even to Inspector rank. Somehow however, along the way that candle had been extinguished. It probably had something to do with what his wife had told him when they'd married twenty years ago. 'Better to be a big fish in a small pool, than a small fish in a big pool'. He realised his limitations now of course that he'd reached 45 years of age. She'd been right and besides, he had four kids to provide for now and another ten years before he could retire.

As he took his slow even stride toward the Inspector's car, he knew that the best thing he could do under the circumstances was to remain a steady worker and keep his nose clean. He'd more than likely then still be in this same job when he retired whilst the Inspector would have long gone onto bigger and better things. The turnover of such officers here was rapid to say the least. Mentally, he gave this one twelve months!

Inspector Peters waited patiently in the driver's seat. He debated whether to poke his nose into the traffic accident but decided against it. His relationship with his fellow CID officer was strained to say the least and he'd already felt in the short time he'd been stationed in Etherton that the locally born officers resented him as an outsider. It was best to not provoke them in their duties, which were adequately undertaken, until such time as he had been better accepted. 'This could' he thought ruefully 'take some time'.

At last he could vaguely make out the stout figure of Sgt Grainger coming towards the car through the fog. As usual, he noted the almost nonchalant gait and the peculiar way he swung his arms like a muscle building gorilla. The Sergeant he noted as he came closer was wearing one of those old fashioned Maigret type raincoats; the sort that moved like stiff cardboard. He tried hard not to smile.

"Good morning sir," said Grainger craning his head down to the level of the Inspector. As he casually swept his hand back through his greying, red hair, a perplexed frown crossed his forehead.

"You'll not have experienced our Avon fogs before," he continued "can get worse than this come December, especially near the river – good time for a spot of eel fishing."

"Really Sergeant. I'll try to remember that" said the

Inspector controlling his patience. "Everything under control?"

"Yes sir. Pity about the Chief Constable though. I always look forward to his visits rare as they are. Local man you see!"

"Of course. I don't wish to appear rude Sergeant but how come you're co-ordinating this accident. Surely its one for traffic?"

Les Grainger pondered this for a moment as if having great difficulty understanding the question. It was deliberate on his part and Dougie Peters knew it.

"First on the scene wasn't I. Like you sir, on my way to work. You'll know I live in Compton and besides the fast response vehicle's already out – pile up on the M5."

So that was what PC Shone meant by shortage of staff. For once it looked like Etherton station was in for a busy day. The Inspector decided to change course in the conversation. At this rate, the day would be over before he got started.

"Is there any way through this mess?" he asked.

"The 'artic's' taken a fence out of some woman's garden. She's a little unhappy but as its already knackered, I reckon you could just squeeze through"

"Who else have you got here from our nick?"

"PC Lawrence and WPC Harrington in the Fiesta on North side and there's a 'sandwich car' from Chelt'nam Southside"

"Right. In that case you better come with me. Have a word with Harrington and ask her to drive your vehicle to the nick when this is all over. I need you, we're short staffed at base. Okay, let's see if you can get me through this pile-up. Move to it Sergeant"

The order was crisp and sharp but it had no effect on Grainger. He worked at one pace and one pace only and Dougie had great difficulty controlling his frustration. Perhaps if he drove fast at the man who was now standing in front of his bonnet beckoning him on, it would instil some life into the robot. It was only a fleeting thought, he didn't want Sgt Grainger to be getting premature retirement on full pay as a result of his action.

Gingerly and with deep concentration the car inched it's way through the fog, its headlights picking out the carnage of blood and twisted metal which the fire officials were hacking away at with their oxyacetylene torches and crowbars. A churned stomach which the Inspector had experienced many times had him gulping in the languid air laced with diesel fumes. The actual sighting of the bloodied car driver's face forced back into the car seat's headrest, lifeless eyes staring at the roof, compelled him to look rapidly away. As his earlier thoughts indicated, it didn't look hopeful despite the attention of the ambulance crew.

The Inspector kept the car in first gear. He was an experienced driver having completed the advanced test at Hendon Police College. There were inches to spare but with Grainger's assistance no damage to the Rover and once through the narrowest of gaps he waited patiently for his assistant.

"Sorry about the delay sir," he said, easing his considerable bulk into the passenger seat. "PC Lawrence wanted to know when he would be relieved. Apparently he's playing soccer against South Wales Police this afternoon and wants to get his head down for a couple of hours."

Peters wondered what the force was coming to when sport took priority over police duties but he didn't think the time was right for such politics.

"What did you tell him?" he asked

"He'd have to do without a kip, we're not running a ruddy kindergarten!"

"Good man." The Inspector conceded that what Les Grainger lacked in ambition was often made up with commonsense.

The journey through the smoggy countryside to Police HQ was uneventful, punctuated only by the frequent crackling of messages passing through on the RT. As they crossed the old Victorian bridge which spanned the River Avon and onto the main Etherton road, they were passed by a squad car in the opposite direction. Its headlights, hazard indicators and blue light were all on full power but they were still inadequate for the seriousness of the weather conditions. Behind the car, seemingly at a snail's pace, was a lorry carrying the heavy duty crane.

"Wouldn't fancy his job!" the Sgt commentated dryly. "Shit this is going to be a right bum day!"

PC Shone pulled his face away from the office window. The tip of his nose was white from the contact with the glass. He turned sharply and in a clear 'Etherton' accent called over to the Desk Sergeant, a balding figure who was talking rapidly into a microphone.

"Sarge, its too late. The Inspector's car just pulled up"

Sgt Denny looked up and rubbed his fingers into the corners of his eyes trying to dislodge the sleep crust.

"You'd better tell him lad" he said. "It'll certainly make his day knowing that the Chief Constable is here and has started his inspection without him."

"But I did try to contact him, he'd already left," the young officer protested.

"You'd might well wish you'd left by the time Inspector Peters has finished with you" came the Sergeant's acid response. He was fiddling for a handkerchief to try and get the sleep crust out of his eye. "And Shone!" he shouted as the constable headed for the door. "This is not one of the best times for your disappearing acts."

Whether PC Shone had intended such a thing was of irrelevance. As he left the confines of the operations room, any such intentions were already too late. Inspector Peters had entered the main entrance and was actively involved in a discussion with Chief Constable Methuen. Noticing the young officer in the background, Peters steely eyes bore into him like a masonry drill attacking a virgin piece of granite. Shone froze to the spot not knowing which way to turn. At that moment his youthful features looked visibly aged.

Chapter Three

The glowing, red, digital inter-face of the clock radio flipped from 8.31 to 8.32 and the darkened room, silent bar the gentle breathing of its occupant was immediately subjected to an orderly and controlled voice.

"And now for the local news on Radio Wyvern. Thick fog has enveloped all areas of Hereford and Worcester, particularly to the south of Worcester in the Vale Of Evesham area. Traffic is restricted to a single lane between Junctions 6 and 7 on the motorway due to an accident on the contra flow system. Drivers are advised to avoid the area if at all possible and on the A435 Cheltenham to Etherton road, the police inform us that the road is blocked just outside the village of Compton. This is due to a lorry losing its load of newsprint and subsequent impact with a car. A five mile tail back has built up and it will be at least 2 hours before the road can be cleared. So the message to drivers' everywhere is 'take care' and is your journey really necessary?"

For Mrs Joyce Mitchell it was a routine start to what was to prove to be a far from routine day. She gingerly tested the temperature of the bedroom by cautiously sliding out an arm from under the duvet, groping for the dressing gown. Her fingers, from years of experience, made contact at the first attempt and she hauled-in the familiar garment.

Now, it was mind over matter. Her worst thoughts were confirmed as the clock told her that if she left it any longer it would be a mad rush to get everything done in the time allotted. She took a deep breath and flung back the duvet. The shock to the system was sufficient to wipe away the last remnants of sleep and quickly now, she wrapped the gown around her.

Whilst waiting for the water from the immersion heater to appear hot at the taps, she took her customary steps across the bathroom to the scales and looked at her reflection in the mirror.

The sunken eyes and greying hair depressed her. Where had the years gone? Where once the green eyes had flirted so successfully at the round bottomed youths, now there was nothing but emptiness. The once dark hair, now lightened through various bottles over the years, lay dank and lifeless. Her figure, which even ten years ago excited Herbert, had spread outwards despite continuous short lived crazes of keep-fit, aerobics, slimming diets and other televised media hypes. She was fifty years old and as her sagging breasts showed through the well-worn blue dressing gown, there was no escaping the fact – she damn well looked fifty years old!

A cursory glance at the scales confirmed her worst fears, another pound up on the previous day. How would she be able to hold her head up at weight watchers that evening? Perhaps she'd ring-in with flu - no that wouldn't do; Alison her partner would be calling for her. God knows why she wanted to go to weight watchers, Alison was positively anorexic as she was! Perhaps it was just an excuse for her to see Herbert?

Joyce dismissed the thought almost as soon as it had crossed her mind. Alison made a pass at anything in trousers. Part and parcel of her being a rich, spoilt wife whose husband was permanently away on overseas business. She was bored of course, not having male company at home made her like a tigress on heat when she got within ten yards of any reasonably good-looking man. And Herbert was still handsome she knew. It was so much easier for a man. Of course he was five years younger than her but surprisingly still had that rounded bottom that she'd fallen in love with. The tailored suits helped but the main reason for his slim build, was the amount of squash he played. To Joyce, it was unnatural. She'd tried playing the game once but Herbert hadn't the patience and her bulky figure made her so clumsy at it that she hadn't bothered since. Herbert however, relished the competitiveness and played regularly twice or even three times a week with his accountancy partner Jeremy Roberts, who as Herbert put it, 'wasn't up to much but being 6 years younger than him, gave him a good run-around'.

After a quick splash of water and a half-hearted few strokes through her limp hair with a brush, Joyce trundled across the landing. She knocked on her son Paul's bedroom door as she approached the top of the L shaped staircase and received the usual grunts from his teenage lips. All seemed as normal and she knew he wouldn't get up until she screamed at him when the breakfast was on the table. Fortunately, the house backed on the River Avon and it would only take him ten minutes to get to his job at Compton Post Office. This was because of the adjacent Compton Ferry, probably the smallest ferry in the world. It consisted of a chain rope slung across the river to a Victorian ratchet-type contraption, which had to be raised or lowered to the riverbed depending on river traffic. In effect, you lugged yourself over in the little craft, which took a maximum of a dozen people, but at this time of year, invariably seldom had more than two. That included the ferryman also!

The beauty of it from Paul's point of view was that if he'd gone by road, he would have had to do over two miles via the Etherton road bridge. This would have played havoc with his early morning lie-in. Like most teenage boys mornings were not his strong point!

The postman arrived on cue as Joyce turned the toast under the grill. As usual all the mail was for Herbert and she placed the letters to the right hand side of the plate bearing his eggcups. Herbert was a creature of habit. Everything had its place and everything had to be in its place. She glanced at the kitchen clock, moved into the breakfast room and switched on the TV. Both the men in the family liked an update on the news. Finally she passed through the door into the hallway and stood at the bottom of the Victorian staircase. Apart from the mahogany fireplace in the lounge, this was the only original craftsmanship left in the modernised old house.

She was about to shout up to them, when she was interrupted by the telephone.

"Etherton 41027," she answered in her smooth manner.

"Ah Mrs Mitchell – its Herbert's secretary Jan"

"Well I must say Jan, you're in the office bright and early. How did you manage it in all this fog?" asked Joyce.

Both ladies were on familiar terms with one another. Indeed Jan's husband Gerald was Herbert's solicitor and the referral's of new business generated between practices was of mutual benefit to both. It was only last week that both Gerald and Jan had dined with them. They were sort of mixing business with pleasure as Herbert had made out a fresh will to which Gerald was the executor!

Jan, like Joyce was plump and in her fifties, so being of the same generation, they found they had similar interests. Jan however had no misgivings about her weight. She was content to accept her middle-age position and enjoyed working for her husband who despite some pressing by Joyce was in her words 'polite, efficient, reliable and hard-working'. If he had a fault it was that he worked too hard and should learn to relax. Joyce countered with the squash being his relaxation and although Jan had agreed that the subject did come up in conversation; being his private secretary Joyce had to accept that it was unlikely that Jan would criticise him. Before she had a further opportunity to question further, Jan had tactfully changed the subject over to Gerald's passion for painting wildlife.

"The fog?" came Jan's baffled response down the line. "To be honest Joyce, I hadn't even realised the weather was bad. I'm telephoning from home, have only just got up and not had an opportunity to look out of the windows yet. We had a little wine last night and you know what it does to me – sort of makes me glow all over. Gerald, the lazy devil is still in bed. I'm taking his breakfast up – he deserves it"

Joyce realised as she listened to the voice on the other end that what Jan was saying, though not in words, was that she had got a little randy on the wine and seduced Gerald. She would never say such a thing. Being on the same wavelength, women's' telepathy was sufficient.

"Really – mine's not up yet either," said Joyce in a voice designed to give a similar impression. This had sufficient effect to break the personal element of the phone call into a business one.

"The reason I called Joyce, is to remind Mr Mitchell of his appointment with the bank concerning Enterprise Transport at 10am this morning. He probably won't forget but he did say the appointment was important and asked me to remind him!"

"I'll see he gets the message Jan. Is that all?"

"Yes thanks. Must dash, I think Gerald's porridge is burning. Bye"

Joyce replaced the receiver. At the bottom of the staircase she took a deep breath before opening her lungs and bellowing in a voice that sounded more in keeping with a fishwife.

"It's a quarter to nine – come and get it!"

Almost instantly she heard a bedroom door open and a set of feet padding across the landing.

"At least Paul's made a move," she thought to herself as she tightened the belt to her dressing gown. It was decidedly chilly. "I'd better put the fire on."

The bars on the electric fire were not even at full heat when Joyce entered the breakfast room via the kitchen carrying the saucepan of boiled eggs. Paul was already halfway through his cornflakes.

"Morning Mum," came the response through a mouthful of flakes. "Where's Dad?"

"Having a lie-in by looks of things. Paul you could at least have combed your hair before breakfast!"

The young lad ignored her. Getting the fuel intake was far more important than appearance at this stage. His mother quickly dipped her hands into the saucepan for the eggs. She hated this bit and always burnt her fingers getting them out.

"Paul did you hear what I said?" she repeated.

This time her son looked up at her and fixed her straight in the eyes. The mop of fine blonde hair travelled up with his head movement, obscuring his right eye. It was a narrow, fresh face that confronted her. The boy was not yet the man despite his 18 years. His cheeks still retained that puffiness associated with childhood. It would surely go as the weekly novelty shave became a daily chore.

"Sorry Mum," he said. "I'll comb it before I go to work – honest."

With that he returned to his cereal and his annoying habit of scraping the bottom of the bowl with the spoon gathering every last drop of milk. The noise forced Joyce to grit her teeth, as she returned to the kitchen with the saucepan.

She poured herself a glass of milk and sipped it. "Where is he?" she thought, her eyes turning to the kitchen clock. Herbert always came down before Paul – perhaps he was ill. She'd better check. Damn the man; the understanding was she would get breakfast and he would look after himself without her running after him. It had been like that for twenty years and she had no intention of upsetting such a routine now.

"Paul – go and check on your Dad will you?" she called from the kitchen.

"But I'll be late!"

"Do as your told," she snapped back.

There was a pause, severe muttering and banging of furniture before the 'clump, clump' up the stairs could be heard. A few seconds later his footsteps could be heard travelling faster down than they had going up.

Paul burst into the kitchen with a puzzled expression on his cherubic face.

"He's not in his bedroom Mum. The bed's not been slept in!"

"What," Joyce's voice was raised in alarm. "But he must be!"

"No Mum." Seeing the startled look in his mother's eyes, he tried to re-assure her. "Perhaps he got up earlier and has already left for the office," he stated.

"No," she said. "He'd never do that. Not leave the house

without telling me. He certainly would not make the bed. Something's wrong."

Disregarding her lack of clothing, she rushed to the front door. Hurriedly she unlocked it and ventured out in the fog onto the tarmac surface of the drive.

The cold, damp, still air seeped through the thin material of her gown causing her nipples to protrude but she didn't feel it. Her heavy, unfit body laboured the short distance to the detached garage so that when she reached it, already she could see the vapour of her exhalation as its warmth came into contact with the cold air. Frantically she grabbed at the metal handle of the double garage doors. Taking a pace backwards, her efforts were rewarded with the swing upwards of the weighted doors. The garage was half empty – no gleaming red Toyota MR6, only her own black mini.

It was full a second before the realisation hit her. Her mind was confused. Who was the client Herbert said he was going to see last night? After twenty years of marriage, such a routine of seeing clients in the evening was too regular an occurrence. Herbert always told her when he was going to be late home so as she did not have to bother with cooking dinner but often she hadn't really taken the information in. At least, not the names anyway! She couldn't think straight as she crossed her arms across her heaving bosom and turned to walk back to the house. Her body now reacted sharply to the weather conditions and she shivered. She could feel dampness on her cheek as a droplet trickled from the corner of her eye.

"Paul – his car's not in the garage either," she heard herself screaming as she burst back through the front door. She was surprised at the hysterical sound of her own voice. It sounded so unnatural.

The gangly youth before her with the puffy cheeks looked lost. He stared vacantly at his mother as she visibly shook in front of him in the hallway. Her face was the same shade of grey as the shirt and trousers that he wore. Paul wanted to move but couldn't. He was a victim of his teenage years and had turned against all the cuddly, touching stuff with his mother.

The lad didn't hate her but emotionally he'd withdrawn from her. It was callous, he knew but as she grew older he found himself getting to dislike her more and more. "When he was young, she was so beautiful," he thought in his mind "now look at her – fat, old, dishevelled and visibly shaking." Such a sight physically sickened him!

"For God's sake get a grip of yourself Mum!" he shouted at her and pushed past to shut out the draught left by the gaping front door.

Joyce looked at her son. She was shocked by his behaviour, so much so that she reacted angrily.

"How dare you talk to me like that," she said, "I'm your mother!"

"Then start acting like it and don't get so bloody hysterical woman. So Dad's missing. There could be a perfectly logical explanation but oh no – you have to put on your centre of attention act. It won't wash with me anymore. I suggest you sit down calmly and think rationally about his movements. Are you sure for example that he didn't say he was staying overnight somewhere?"

Paul knew this was a long shot. His father seldom had to make business trips of such a lengthy distance as to require an overnight stop.

"Of course not," said his mother.

"Right." Paul at least was now beginning to gather his thoughts. "In that case, I suggest you ring the office first and check that he's not there and have a word with Mr Roberts to discover who he was supposed to visit last night. If Dad's not at the office ... telephone the evening client, whoever he was and see if he turned up. Finally ..." Paul stopped speaking – he'd recalled something.

"Mr Hagan," he said. "Of course, I remember now!"

"Mr Hagan?" asked Joyce trying desperately to fathom out what her soon meant.

"Old Mr Hagan – my employer that's who. I recall in the

post office yesterday, that he said my father was coming over last night and that Dad had promised to have a chat with him – something to do with Capital Gains Tax on a property he'd sold. Look Mum I'm late as it is. I'll nip over to work now and check to see if Dad called last night. You ring the office and check and I'll telephone you from the post office. Now come on – pull yourself together, he'll be alright."

Joyce looked at her son. This was unlike him to be so confident and in control of the situation. Normally he was withdrawn, quiet and unassuming. What had come over him? He had intelligence but was lazy which is why he did not pass exams at school and had ended up working in a village post office. His character had changed almost overnight. It gave her a strange feeling.

"Yes-ye-s, of course," she stuttered but already he had gone.

Her hands were shaking as she picked up the receiver to the telephone and began to punch out the digits.

Sgt. Denny pounded up the stairs two at a time. Being the Desk Sergeant at Etherton Police Station HQ, it was about the only exercise he ever got apart from playing skittles for a local pub side that is.

Reaching the top of the thirty-one steps, he was pleased to note that he was not out of breath and as a reward he tentatively tapped his portly stomach.

"Nice one Sarge"

"Where do you think your going Almond? Shouldn't you be over at the nightclub – eh what's its name?"

"Justine's' sarge. I'm on my way now. Just checking with CID – don't want to tread on any toes."

"Right lad – on your way then!"

"Smart arse," thought Sgt Denny to himself. he didn't particularly like PC Anthony Almond. PC Shone was bad enough with his eye for the ladies and his habit of being everywhere but where he should be. Almond however was in a class of his own. It was now 10.00am and it was the first time he'd seen him today. He hadn't quite worked the man out despite the fact Almond had now been at Etherton for six months.

PC Almond was an enigma. Top recruit at Hendon, highly assessed by his course officers and presumably destined for higher rank but it was difficult to discover what made him 'tick'. Since he'd been at Etherton, he'd appeared edgy – didn't mix with the other officers and was to all intents and purposes a loner. Always polite and with a willing smile, Sgt Denny still nursed doubts about him. He wasn't prejudiced, but rare though black officers were within the police force PC Almond would have to work much harder if he was to win favour with Sgt Denny.

"Come in," gruffed the voice from behind the door marked 'Inspector Peters'.

"Ah Bob what can I do for you?" said Les Grainger looking up from behind a desk stacked high with files.

"I was looking for the Inspector"

"He's doing the rounds with the big-wig," Les Grainger leant back in the chair so that it was tilted on two legs. Laughingly, he lifted his legs onto the desk.

"You'll have to do with the organ grinder's monkey instead," he said.

"Has PC Almond been to see you?"

"Yep – I've just cleared him to go round to Justine's' and get statements on the nightclub fracas. Wasn't too serious was it?"

"Nah – usual drunken fighting, complaints of urinating and noise. One chap had a glass thrust into his face. About par for the course. When my lads got there, it was all over bar the shouting" said Sgt Denny taking a seat opposite the Detective Sergeant.

"That's not what I've come up for Les," he said. "It may be something or nothing but I've just taken a call from a Mrs Mitchell. Her husband didn't come home last night and his car's not in the garage."

"So"

"Yes I know twenty-four hours have not passed and guys

often up and leave their missus but this one sounds different. Firstly he's an accountant, very routine sort of fellow; went to see a client last evening and not been seen since. Respected, married 20 years, nice house down by the river. I'm just putting you in the picture."

"Yes of course Bob. I'll make a note. Keep me informed won't you. What have you done so far?"

"Sent a WPC round to see her, get a photograph – that sort of thing."

Sgt Grainger chewed on the end of a pencil and thought for a moment. Whilst contemplating the information imparted to him, his other hand absent mindedly fingered his red hair. Presently he said

"You know Bob that's all we need today. Got the Big-Wig on inspection, a fatal road smash, a burglary that's just hit my desk, short staffed, problems at the nightclub and up to our eyeballs in fog. This place is going mad. It used to be so damn quiet here before our precious new Inspector arrived. What the hell's going on? All we damn well need now is a murder and we'll really be in the big time!"

Chapter Four

'Greaves to Law – Law to Best – a delightful little shimmy past the defender there. This packed Wembley crowd are certainly getting their Cup Final monies worth of entertainment as Best takes it on, does a one-two wall pass with Pele and carries the ball down near the sideline. A great low cross across the penalty area and there, diving in bravely with his head is Barker and it's a ....'

'Beep, beep, beep, beep, beep'

The prone figure lying on his stomach, with an arm dangling surreptitiously alongside the bedroom carpet, opened an eye. Sub-consciously his mouth moved into gear.

"Go-al"

Immediately, the light-sensitive digital clock projected the figures 0830am onto the ceiling and Gary Barker twisted over on his back to read them.

"What the hell is the alarm doing going off an hour early," he thought to himself. It wasn't often now, at the age of 38 that he had a return of his boyhood dreams of scoring a goal in the English FA Cup Final at Wembley. The fact that this modern day gadget had apparently malfunctioned, before he could receive the applause of the spectators and legendary players had ruined his start to the day.

He reached for the bedside table light and switched it on. The soft lighting illuminated his side of the bedroom, which was painted a pastel shade of green with the exception of the wall against which the head of the bed rested. It was 'designer label' bedroom gear for the Eighties and although he'd gone along with it at the time, he had to admit it wasn't really his scene.

He picked up his chunky gold wristwatch and double-checked the time before clasping it onto his wrist. The watch contrasted well with the coffee coloured tone of his skin.

The figure next to him stirred and a sleepy, barely audible voice murmured, "Gary."

He turned his eyes towards her and the billowing black hair draped over the black satined duvet. At least the 'mix and match' pattern worked on the bed linen.

Gary rolled over onto his side to face her, sliding an arm under the covers and onto the raised, rounded buttocks.

This girl Jacky, was a total contrast to Karen* his last, but already after six months she had him organised. Karen had been a typical blonde English Rose, thirteen years his younger with a freshness to match. She'd been a nurse at Main City Hospital and had helped him on his first case on his return to his homeland England after ten years in America. He smiled as he remembered how she'd rescued him at Heathrow after being mugged and then again in hospital after he'd 'come round' after a car crash. He'd never forget those first moments and for a time after that murder case, a long term relationship looked a probability. Things never worked out the way they are planned though. Before long their lifestyles clashed. She could not accept the unorthodox hours involved in the detective line of business and he in turn found it impossible to live with a woman who was forever on night shifts and talking about patients 'medical conditions' in the time they did manage together. Such subjects nauseated him and they were already growing apart when Karen had an opportunity to nurse in America. He'd not stood in her way and they'd parted on friendly terms. That had been a year ago and they still exchanged letters. To begin with he missed her terribly but his agency, now two years old, was coming into its own – so much so, that he now had a partner Jason Lear, a man like himself of mixed origins. Jason was white, a Celt of Scots, Irish and Welsh extraction whilst he was coloured, of English stock on his mother's side and West Indian/Asian on his fathers. His

* See 'Dead Beat'

mother was dead – murdered! He'd never got on with her; she'd been a lady of loose morals. The brutal murder had sickened him though and it was the solving of that case that led him to setting up GB Private Investigations.

His father, he'd never known. He'd done a runner as soon as Janet his mother, had got pregnant. All he knew was that he'd been called Henry. Janet had married a wealthy publisher named George and he had treated Gary as if he were his own son. Gary was grateful to him for that but as soon as he was old enough, he'd left home to make his own way in life.

He'd had a half sister Elizabeth who too had been murdered in the same case. Ironically, he'd come back from America to see her, only to arrive too late. Now, with the exception of George who he occasionally checked on, he had no family, so that once Karen had left for America, for months he'd been lonely and it had only been the agency that had kept his sanity.

During the period between Karen's departure and Jacky's arrival, he'd thrown everything into GB Private Investigations. He'd taken on all cases, including the laborious 'leg-work' involved in cases of adultery. It meant nights of keeping watch in cars on illicit affairs but even that was more preferable to tracing missing persons. In these cases, the people concerned invariably turned up but the 'clients' forgot to inform him. This always led to an argument over fees. Divorce work might be boring but at least it paid well and in the case of Jacky it had its compensations. They'd met as a result of him tailing her. What had originally been a routine case of a rich, suspicious husband checking up on his wife, did in fact end up in the divorce courts. His suspicions had initially proved unfounded but the hunter had become in the end, the hunted. Adultery had been proved – Gary was named in court as co-respondent!

"Ga-ry," the sensuous murmur came again at his side. "Are you going to stroke my arse all night or can I expect something a little more adventurous."

The cat was purring now. The eyes were still closed but the lips were moist and inviting.

What was a fellow to do in such circumstances? Right – stop messing about and get stuck in!

Gary's hand slid effortlessly from the softness of her buttocks along the silky smooth channel of her spine towards her shoulder blades. At the same time, his mouth plunged hurriedly to the parted lips. Jacky shifted her position so that in the half-light he got a magnificent 'eyeball' of her heaving breasts which at that angle made them look larger than they really were. His lips and hands now urgently changed direction and concentrated wholly on the voluptuous assets. Her aroused nipples protruded further and further into his mouth and their respective private parts responded as they thrust together.

Both bodies that seconds before had been relaxed, now pulsated with earthy, physical desire. Tongues darted, hands and fingers caressed erogenous zones until excitement from both partners could be contained no longer.

Jacky widened her legs as the open invitation for her lover to mount her and on the penetrating thrust she raised her hips in order to accommodate and further excite him. She knew how much he liked that.

"Dig deep my darling." Her voice had a throaty huskiness as she spoke.

"Harder, harder – oh yes that's so fucking good."

It was hungry lust now as they both searched for the others' fluids. There respective brown and white bodies glowed with the exertions as the pleasure was enhanced.

Each of them was fast approaching the obliviousness of their attempts to make it pleasurable for the other. Gary thrust harder and harder, faster and faster, like the workings of a piston engine in a chamber. She in turn raised her hips with each mounted thrust into the cutting.

Her vocabulary gushed as Gary reached the point of no return.

"Give it me babe, give it me babe – yes – now, I'm ready"

There was a final flourish from the dominant male as he ground into her with the deepest of all thrusts and then she felt his arms grip her shoulders so tightly that she could feel her shoulder blades being compressed into her body but then the warm feeling arrived. It came from him in a rush that temporarily surprised her but almost immediately the same ecstatic pleasure swallowed her up and both of them bathed in the aura of sensuality.

"That," said Gary emphatically after his heartbeat had returned somewhere near normality "was really something. What a way to start they day. I don't suppose you planned this?"

She waited until he had rolled off her before saying

"I thought that making love first thing in the morning would make a change that's all." Jacky pulled up the duvet to cover her breasts. As her body temperature dropped, she could feel the November chill.

Gary raised himself onto his elbow and looked down at her face. The exertion of their lovemaking had brought a rosey colour to her creamy complexion.

"So you did change the alarm," he said in a teasing manner.

"Of course. I wanted to start my day with my very own Private Dick!" she said laughingly.

Gary laughed too. He liked a dame who was polite in public but talked dirty in bed.

"You want to be careful," he said, "you might get more than you bargained for"

She gave him a sultry look with pouting lips. Her green eyes opened wider and the long half-mooned eyebrows lifted.

"You reckon your *up* to it already?" she asked and her hand slipped down the bed and over his thighs.

Gary clasped her hand before it reached its intended target. At the same time he could hear the sound of the telephone in the hallway.

"Saved by the bell," he said as he quickly slipped out from underneath the duvet and padded over towards the wardrobe and his dressing robe.

Jacky's eyes followed his naked rear and her tongue circumnavigated the top layer of her teeth in approval. He had a firm taut bum, narrow waist and firm shoulder muscles. In the half-light, he looked darker than he really was. She caught a glimpse of his manhood whilst he half-turned in the process of tying the robe. Even now, she decided he was what you could term 'well-hung'. The physique of the man pushing forty was commendable. Not an inch of excess fat anywhere. In fact, if it wasn't for the steel grey head of hair, he could pass for a man ten years younger. She decided she really liked this man – he was a winner and they were hard to find these days.

Gary could feel her eyes on him as he left the bedroom and moved easily into the hallway of the flat. The woman was getting under his skin – that he knew. He could, if he wasn't careful, get seriously involved with her. In contrast to Karen, she was an experienced, mature thirty year old who knew what turned a man on and took enormous pleasure in being able to control him. Damn her, he only had to brush past her and he was aroused. That hadn't happened since he was a teenager and had been virtually seduced over a table tennis table in a recreation room at an athletic club. The girl had calmly locked the door behind her and as near as damn well raped him. It had been a short and quick experience then and here he was twenty years later with a sex hungry divorcee. The trouble was he liked it too much – not just the body although that was one hell of an exciting thing in itself but Jacky too. She was in control of the relationship, was not demanding in an emotional capacity and always sensed his mood. Knowing when to speak and when not was an art and she certainly had that.

"Gary Barker," he grunted into the Mickey Mouse receiver. It was a relic from his years in America and proved to visitors to his flat that he had a sense of humour.

"Morning boss," came the clipped tones of his younger detective partner Jason Lear. "How goes it?"

"Good god. If your at the office at this hour then all I can say is that your TV set must be on the blink" came Gary's sarcastic response. He knew that his ex Harrow friend was an addict of all night 'junk' television which invariably meant he was late arriving at their 'no expense spared' offices above a Chinese takeaway in the Main Broadway city centre.

"Hardly old chap," came Jason's response. "Had a little shindig at one of my ex-girlfriends' place. Tried to get a thing going with her again and was forced to sleep on the sofa. You know how I love my creature comforts. Couldn't sleep so came straight in. Just as well I did really. Had a phone call from someone called Mrs Mitchell. She seemed desperate to contact you personally."

"Mrs Mitchell?" Gary racked his photographic memory but the name did not register anything out of the ordinary. "What did she want?"

"Wouldn't say Gaza old chum. Asked you to call her urgently. Gave her number as Etherton 41027. Lord knows where that is!"

"OK Jason. I'll get back to you. In the meantime, don't forget you've got that bailiff's warrant to execute today."

"Shit," came the response. It was unusual for Jason to swear and as if realising it he added "sorry about that." You know how I hate these things especially when it involves people who move in similar circles to myself. Why did we take on this type of work for goodness sake?"

"Because it pays your champagne bill," said Gary, mimicking his cultured accent and he replaced the receiver. Nonchalantly he reached for the dialling code directory adjacent to the telephone and flipped through the slim volume until he found Etherton, Worcs. Still confused, as he was certain that he knew nobody from the 'Shires' that far west, he again lifted the receiver and dialled.

The voice at the other end answered on the first ring and it sounded very agitated as if starved for information.

"Yes what is it?" it said "have you any news?"

"Mrs Mitchell?" Gary enquired

"Yes"

"Gary Barker of GB Private Investigations – you telephoned my partner at our Main office!"

"Yes, yes of course. Thank you for ringing so promptly. Its my husband – he's missing!"

Gary kept his voice calm and controlled. It wasn't the first time he'd had an hysterical woman on the line.

"You'll have to enlighten me Mrs Mitchell," he said. "Please take your time and go back to the beginning."

He listened attentively as the story unravelled in fractured sentences so that although he did not have a complete picture, he at least had the gist of it. When she'd finished her frantic explanation he began asking positive questions.

"Your husband would be the accountant Herbert Mitchell?" he asked.

"Yes"

"Of Mitchell and Roberts?"

"Yes"

His photographic memory now worked fast. He remembered the man and pictured him. Tall, lean, mid-forties. He was an easy going fellow with a ready smile. Comparatively good looking but not he sort of person to which women instantly responded. His main redeeming features were the Woody Allen type glasses. They gave him the look of an intellectual he recalled.

Gary remembered how their paths had crossed. It was some time ago now, when he'd first started his business here in Main. he'd not even considered the book-keeping side of the business then, been to busy trying to get clients!

He'd been hired as additional cover for some pop star or other at one of the prestige city hotels and whilst his protégé was sleeping off his previous night's concert, Gary had popped into the hotel bar for a drink. Mister Herbert Mitchell had been propping up the same bar. Apparently he'd been invited to give a talk at a seminar in the hotel to do with tax havens. They'd chatted and the accountant had given him some useful advice and a name of a local accountant who he understood specialised in Gary's line of work. By contrast Gary had returned the favour by giving him one of his freshly printed GB Private Investigation cards. He even remembered his closing words as he'd left Mr Mitchell and returned to his boring assignment.

"You never know when you might need a confidential agent," he'd said. Advertising did work and now he was being given the opportunity to make it pay.

"Have you informed the police?" he asked Mrs Mitchell

"Yes. Actually when you rang I thought it might be them"

"What did they say?"

"They weren't any help. By all accounts he has to be missing for 24 hours or something"

"I see"

"You will help won't you?" The desperate tinge was in her voice again.

"That depends Mrs Mitchell. I have to say it could prove expensive"

He hated mentioning money at such a time but the subject had to be broached

"Oh ple-ase Mr Barker," she pleaded. "Herbert obviously thought you were good at your job. I've been going through his things and he would not have kept your card if he felt that you were not professional in your line of work, as he was in his"

Gary thought for a moment. He could do with a change of scenery and anyhow, the man had not taken a fee for his advice which had proved to be invaluable. The accountant he'd recommended, not only saved him money but had put a lot of business Gary's way. In addition he'd proved to be a good friend. The least he could do under the circumstances was to help this missing man's wife – it was the professional thing to do.

"I'll be there this afternoon Mrs Mitchell – I promise. Give me your address!"

Jacky was fixing her suspenders when he returned to the bedroom. Her pure white lacy bra and French knickers contrasted well with her cascading black hair and creamy textured skin.

Gary was blunt.

"I'm going away for a few days," he said

"Great, I could do with a break – where are we going?"

"I said I was going – not we!" he emphasised. "A friend of mine has gone missing"

"Where?" she asked. Her voice showed consideration for the importance of his work.

"A small market town in Worcestershire – Etherton. Have you ever heard of it?"

"Well yes. It's a fruit farming area. Very popular with tourists and not far from Chelters"

"Chelters?"

"Cheltenham Spa," she said noticing his inquisitive look. "Regency buildings, rich people and a well known horse racing track." Gary knew Cheltenham of course. He'd just never heard the term 'Chelters'.

"When were you ever there?" he asked

"My ex husband was born in Chelters I'll have you know. You're shacked up with classy breeding!" She laughed. It was the sort of girlish laugh that made rugged men go weak at the knees.

Gary felt hurt. He did not appreciate hearing her talk about the men in her life.

"Fascinating," he said moodily and reached into the wardrobe for his jeans.

****

He watched her from the window in the lounge. The flat was on the third floor of a tower block on the outskirts of Main and it afforded an excellent birds' eye view.

She was fashionably dressed in a knee length white leather coat, similar in style to the old raincoats that popped up in the Black and White TV Maigret series and the accessories were knee length boots with stiletto heel and a pill box hat – both in matching white. It was again 'designer label'. On a grey

November morning, even from this height and distance she looked a beauty as she jauntily swaggered over to the Golf GTI. He stayed transfixed until the car disappeared on its way to her own apartment where she had her very own art studio. Her ex-husband provided well for her and she had ambitions in the field of illustrations for books. She hadn't as yet been commissioned but Gary had seen her portfolio and with her looks, personality and talent – it was only a question of time.

After she'd gone, he hurriedly shaved, dressed and threw a few clothes into a holdall before returning the call to his office where he updated Jason on his current caseload. Jason was a little 'put out' about the short notice of his leave of absence but as the case looked likely to be highly profitable he was easily won over. If there was one thing that Jason Lear liked more than women, it was a thick wad of 'spondulicks'.

45 minutes after leaving the warmth and scent of Jacky's body, the black SAAB Turbo was purring at a steady 70mph along the motorway towards Oxford. One minute later, the car was careering from the fast lane, across the motorway and heading for the hard shoulder and a tree-lined embankment. The driver was seen fighting the wheel every inch of the way!

Chapter Five

"Susie! Why the hell is the bloody sprout lorry still stuck in the yard. Where's bloody Mack?"

The enormous bull-like frame of Patrick Wainwright, all but blocked the daylight of the entrance doorway to the dingy office that represented the nub of Enterprise Transport's operations.

Its solitary female occupant sat behind a makeshift stained counter, looked a fragile thing, at first glance, like a very delicate china doll that would break at the slightest touch.

The sudden bursting entrance of the Managing Director showed however that she was made of sterner stuff.

"He's gone to scrounge another wagon from Vic Massons," she said calmly, as she picked up the scattered bits of paper which had been lifted by the draught of her boss's entrance.

"And what's wrong with our truck?" Wainwright demanded in his brash manner. "No – don't tell me – let me guess!" He kicked the door shut behind him, lifted the counter hatch and proceeded towards the coffee percolator. Having poured himself a cup, he took a sip and stood intimidatingly behind the pencil-thin slip of a girl who was now in the process of feeding a sheet of headed notepaper in the typewriter.

Susan Key his secretary and general dogsbody could feel his hot breath on her neck as he crouched by her shoulder. She knew he was trying to look down her 'V' necked sweater. Why he bothered she didn't really know – she certainly never encouraged him and besides it wasn't as if she had anything worth his interest. Yet, he'd start every day in the same manner. Burst into the office cursing and swearing; then the coffee and finally the casual, almost tender grip on her shoulders.

His voice was calmer now, almost controlled.

"It's the damn gearbox again isn't it love?"

"Yes Mr Wainwright," she said blandly "only this time the whole thing has dropped out!" Susie said nothing. She was used to this sort of language. it was second nature to her now, being the only woman in the midst of a male dominated trucking environment. Provided the men didn't grope her and her pay packet was in her hand every Friday, she could more than handle it.

She felt the grip on her shoulders relax and watched his powerful frame out of the corner of her heavily mascaraed eye, as he shuffled over to his desk and flopped into the swivelled-back leather chair. It was the only decent piece of furniture in the room. She swung her skinny legs around to face him, taking care not to show too much thigh in her tight black mini skirt. The man looked as though he was carrying the whole world on his shoulders. Sunken eyes, unshaven face, greasy unkempt hair that needed cutting – the man was a mess. Her MD was 35 years of age but the worries drawn across his temple added another five years. Even the plain ring dangling from an earlobe like those worn by gypsies couldn't disguise that.

Patrick Wainwright realised he was being watched but didn't care. As a woman, Susie did not interest him. Apart from the fact she was barely in her twenties and was too skinny by half, he had more than enough problems in that department with the woman he was currently involved with. She was giving him a hard time – which together with the 'dicky' state of his business was pressure enough.

He yanked hard at the bottom drawer of the desk, sending empty used paper coffee cups flying and reached in for the bottle of whisky. As he poured a generous measure into the black coffee, he said in his broad Brummie accent

"Any more bad news?"

"Mitchell and Roberts rang"

"And?"

"The exact words were Mr Mitchell is indisposed and will not be able to keep his appointment with you today"

"What!" Wainwright exploded. "Two bloody weeks I've waited for that effing accountant to come up with a cash flow projection forecast for the bank and even now he can't come up with the figures. What the hell's that damn firm up to god I pay them enough" He rapidly checked his telephone address reckoner and dialled. Whilst he was waiting he took a slug direct from the whisky bottle. His young assistant returned to her typewriter and began bashing away on a letter.

His conversation was brief and gave no indication who he was talking to.

"Meet me at the Compton Arms for lunch. Its urgent!" he said.

On replacing the receiver, he unlocked the top drawer of his desk and pulled out the company cheque book and latest bank statement. For the next half an hour he poured over his ledgers, working frantically at his calculator, checking and cross checking the financial state of affairs. Finally he leant back in the chair and thought for a few moments before calling over to Susie.

"I've made a list of companies who owe us money. I want you to ring around this afternoon threatening them with the bailiff if the money's not here by the end of the week. Understand?"

"But I did that yesterday Mr Wainwright!" came the girl's response. She was beginning to think that the weekly pay packet might not be around much longer.

"Don't argue lass – do it again. Listen, I shall be out for the rest of the day. Tell Mack its imperative he deliver those sprouts today and it's COD. Has Toby gone on the French run alright?" he questioned.

"Yes. I've got the docking sheet here – 6 barrels of Brennards Ale. There's a note saying he left at 5.30am."

"Good. At least something has gone right today. Got any money in Petty Cash?"

"I think so"

"Give me twenty love." For once he smiled. It was a full-blown affair that gave a hint of a once cheeky nature. "For business expenses" he added.

No sooner had he left the office with the notes stuffed in his jeans than he returned. He stood with his head thrust round the doorway, his hands working feverishly at the zip to his black leather bomber jacket. The smile was there again.

"Don't worry," he said. It'll all work out I promise. Sorry about the language"

After he'd gone Susie went over to his desk to clear away the cups and balls of paper that he'd screwed up. She couldn't help but notice that he'd left a bank statement there.

A puzzled frown crossed her elf-like face. Contradicting what he'd just said, she could not understand why the account was £15,000 in *credit*.

****

The Compton Arms did a lively lunchtime trade, mainly in the public bar by way of bar snacks. There was little option here for Senor Stephano to show off his Spanish catering cuisine and it was left to his wife Maria to appease the hungry workers with their pie and chips. Much of the pub's business came from the nearby Industrial Trading Estate but the smaller, intimate lounge catered for the Spartan number of business management people and it was here that the diminutive pub landlord could work to impress them by improving his English.

"Senor Wainwright," he said, grateful for the opportunity of having someone enter his near empty room. "How are you sir?"

Patrick paused near the entrance inside the lounge. He always found it difficult to adjust his eyes to the over indulgence of lighting. It was like someone popping a camera flash bulb immediately in front of you.

"Ah Stephano," he said, strutting forward past the empty

veneered tables towards the bar. It too was made of the same cheap imitation material, but like most people he didn't notice it.

"Make it a whisky," he said officiously on reaching it.

The Spaniard looked past him and nodded in the direction of the corner alcove. His previously warm welcome now turned sour.

"She's been waiting for perhaps twenty minutes and appears edgy senor," he said.

Patrick glanced in the direction indicated at the elegant, petite figure. Even at this distance she looked a classy lady. Dressed in a pale lemon cashmere dress, cut just above the knee, she appeared cool and confident. Only the steely glint in her eyes as they met his, gave any sign that her mood was suspect.

"Better make it two whiskies," he said to Stephano. "One on the rocks for Mrs Roberts."

Whilst waiting for the drinks he looked at her again. She had tied her long blonde hair back into a bun, which hardened her facial features. Patrick knew this was a bad sign. The state of her hair reflected her moods. When it was long and flowing free, she'd be flirtatious – even sexy but when it was up, she'd be aggressive, efficient and unyielding. This was to be no loving meeting!

He paid for the drinks and ordered two steaks not noticing the angry expression that was building up inside the Spaniard. He didn't care a fart for the greasy little foreigner – anyway the guy was well paid, what more did he want? Besides he had more important things on his mind – like what was eating his lady?

She didn't look up as he placed the drink in front of her but waited for him to make the first move.

"Candy!" he said almost apologetically and quietly for a big man who was more used to barking at people. "What gives?"

She snapped back at him.

"I've told you before, it's not safe for us to meet here. If

Jeremy finds out the whole operation could be jeopardised. I don't like being given orders – *by anyone*" she stressed.

"Nobody knows," he said trying to reason with her.

Only now did she look up from her glass. Her eyes grew wider and the nostrils flared, which gave her a leonine appearance. The voice was raised an octave.

"And what about our Spanish friend?" she demanded.

"Business," he said floundering "he thinks its business."

"I'm not so sure," she replied. "The runt is not to be trusted. He may have to be dealt with."

"Dealt with?" Patrick said with alarm. "What do you mean dealt with?"

"Never mind. It'll hold. Now what's so damned urgent?"

"You told me to let you know if anything out of the ordinary occurred"

"So?"

"Well it ties in with your husband and I'm bloody fed up with Mitchell and Roberts as my accountants. You recommended them if you remember?"

"I thought," she said smilingly putting on the charm "that it would give us a legitimate reason to be seen together"

"Yes I know but their inefficiency is affecting my legitimate business. Mr Mitchell was supposed to have an appointment with me but ………"

"He didn't turn up!" Candy finished the question for him. "The reason he did not arrive is because he's gone missing. My husband phoned me at home. Apparently Joyce Mitchell telephoned in to say he'd not returned home last night. Look Patrick, I'll have a word with Jeremy and get him to call you"

"Is that wise?"

"You're not getting paranoic are you?"

"Well it's just that it might seem suspicious if you were to mention that we'd met"

"Jeremy trusts me implicitly darling," she said, covering his hand with hers over the table. "Besides I shall just say that you'd tried to contact him at our house and I'm passing the message on. You do trust me don't you?"

Candy Roberts was no fool. She was a master at manipulating men and as she turned actress, her face melted into a school-girlish freshness. The bull of a man opposite her was instantly besotted – so much so that he did not even realise that the hand had been removed from his. The expression had reverted in the split second available to her as Senor Stephano served the steaks for lunch.

Chapter Six

Inspector Peters gingerly twisted the business card between the spaces in his fingers, flicking it over from one to the other and back again like an experienced gambler might do with a playing card. He had a lot on his mind, not least of which was the criticisms still ringing in his ears from the recently departed Chief Constable.

He wished he was back in Main doing real police work instead of having to check on petty regulatory matters like station standing orders, registers and the discipline/morale of his officers.

From his office window he looked out across the football pitch to the River Avon beyond. The fog had now mercifully lifted to reveal the brown swirling waters, which were threatening the pitch itself. It was raining again for the third time in as many days and the river had burst its banks and completely immersed the footpath which in the summer months would be alive with the Birmingham day trippers. Now though there was little of interest apart from the debris being swept along with the current.

Presently he stopped doing the manipulative card trick and moved across his cramped office to his raincoat where he extracted a packet of mints. Since giving up smoking on doctors orders some years before, he was now up to two packs a day of the ones with the holes in.

The mint had all but disappeared by the time he lifted the white telephone, which was connected to the control room.

"Sergeant Denny?" He checked until hearing his voice. "If WPC Harrington is there, would you ask her to come up please!"

He'd almost demolished another mint by the time the officer knocked at his door.

"Ah WPC Harrington," he said looking up as the uniformed officer entered. "Take a seat"

She was a pleasant girl he thought – a little overweight but with a homely face, well suited for consoling those that became mixed up in police matters. As she sat there facing him, he could tell she was worrying as ambitious people do. There's always a slight guilt feeling when confronted one to one with a senior officer. He decided to put her at ease.

"Nothing to worry about Harrington. Its this business card!" he said and placed the card in front of her.

"Tell me about your visit to Mrs Mitchell this morning?" he ordered. "How did she strike you?"

"Upset naturally sir, as any woman who loves her husband is when he goes missing"

"Go on"

"Well she seemed totally lost – no confused is a better word. As you are probably aware Mr Mitchell is the senior partner of Mitchell and Roberts Accountants in the High Street. She's spoken of course with his office but nobody has heard anything from him since yesterday. I explained our policy concerning missing people and she thrust this card in my hand saying she couldn't wait – wanted something active and constructive to happen. She said she found the card in one of his suits and has telephoned these people. I understand someone will be arriving later today"

"Anything else"

"No sir. She has a son Paul, who's eighteen and works at Compton Post Office. He's aware his father is missing. I don't think she'll do anything silly and I'll look in again on her on my way home this evening. Its not too far out of my way"

"Good. Here have a mint"

The young officer looked astonished but she took one anyway. Seeing as the inspector appeared to be in a good mood she ventured a question.

"Sir. I wonder whether I could ask you to contribute to a charitable cause?"

"Which one?" Peters gruffed. It wasn't that he was anti charity, it was because ever since he'd arrived in Etherton he'd been digging into his pocket for too many good causes.

"You may remember sir from the local paper the young girl who died recently from leukaemia. The Mayor has set up a fund and I've been nominated as our station's representative"

Peters did not hesitate. His hand was already searching in his back pocket for his wallet. She had been such a pretty girl and it had touched him dearly.

"Yes of course," he said. "I didn't mean to sound so heartless" and he handed over a note. "Let me know if any of our staff need a 'gee-up' to boost the kitty"? he added smiling. "I know some of them can be a tight lot."

After Harrington had left his office, he again picked up the card and re read the words "GB Private Investigations – Proprietor Gary Barker." He'd often wondered what had happened to the fellow who'd interfered on that murder case back in Main. He thought perhaps he might have returned to the States where he had a business but if, as appeared likely, Mr Barker was to appear on his patch again – this time, he'd ensure that the affable 'half breed' did not step out of line. In short, everything as the Chief Constable kept insisting, would be done in accordance with Police Regulations.

He looked at his watch. It was 2pm. The paperwork could wait he decided; some fresh air would do him good.

On his way out of the station he looked in on the control room.

"Shone," he bawled. "Stop fooling around lad. If you've nothing better to do than make paper aeroplanes you can get out on the beat."

PC Shone had not seen the inspector coming and his clean-cut features now blushed red.

Peters continued. "Rather than have you in my office on report lad, I shall check with WPC Harrington to make sure you've made a generous contribution. Do I make myself clear?"

"Yes sir"

"Good. Tell Sgt Denny wherever he's lurking, I've gone into town to see the firm of Mitchell and Roberts. Do you think you can manage that?"

"Yes sir," Shone said humbly.

The Inspector smiled and pulled on his raincoat. 'Hit 'em where it hurts he thought to himself 'in their pockets'. He stepped out into the dismal gloom of a damp November afternoon.

****

"Inspector Peters. Do come in!" Jeremy Roberts gestured by way of his arm a comfortable leather armchair. "Have you met my wife Candy?"

"How do you do Mrs Roberts. I hope I'm not interrupting!" Peters stared straight at her. It was difficult not to and he appreciated he was in the room with a very special lady. It wasn't just her beauty, which was exceptional in itself, but a certain electricity. This was the sort of lady that made strong men wilt at the knees and he was having difficulty concentrating on anything other than her.

Candy Roberts was well aware of her effect on men and played it to her full advantage.

"My pleasure," she said. Her voice was smooth and velvety and the proffered hand had a silk-like quality. "Have you come about Herbert?" she asked. Her palest of blue eyes never left his. She knew instantly that she was winning him over to her side.

"Ye-s," said Peters. He was fighting to maintain his line of reasoning. "May I ask how well you knew him?"

"Quite well Inspector." Candy laughed and Peters felt

uncomfortable. When she laughed, her generous mouth revealed a set of perfectly even teeth.

"My wife as you will have gathered Inspector has an unusual sense of humour" interjected Jeremy Roberts.

"Oh darling," said Candy. "I was only teasing. Look I must dash! Don't forget to make an appointment to see Mr Wainwright. He sounded quite angry on the phone. Oh and what time can I expect you home this evening?"

Jeremy Roberts looked embarrassed. Inspector Peters thought that this was something that often occurred having such a blonde bombshell as Candy for a wife. He felt sorry for the guy and grateful for an ordinary woman like Angela. She might not be Miss World but at least she never showed him up like this girl.

"I'll ring and let you know," Jeremy said lamely.

"Good. Bye darling and you too Inspector. Hope we'll meet again real soon!"

Both men waited and stood with their eyes fixed on Candy's disappearing long legs as she walked along the corridor outside the office.

Eventually Mr Roberts closed the door and ushered the Inspector back to the armchair.

"Sorry about that," he said "she can be a bit of a handful!"

Peters studied the accountant as he made his way towards a sideboard containing a mixture of leader branded spirits.

As with most professional men - image was important. The client expected to see a stereotyped, glossy, expensive example to match the high fees that they were paying. In this respect Mr Jeremy Roberts lived up to that image.

He wasn't that tall, perhaps 5ft 7ins and yet the traditional pin stripe with matching waistcoat made him appear taller. It was an optical illusion in keeping with the taste of the surrounding. Everything looked the genuine thing but closer examination would reveal otherwise. The Dali on the wall – a copy. The leather furniture – vinyl imitation. Even the man himself with a full head of black curly hair – sported a well concealed hairpiece. To the unsuspecting client who perhaps only met his accountant once a year, these things would not be noticed. To Dougie Peters, it was these observations that aroused suspicions. Accountants he knew made a good living. Apart from his obviously expensive wife, where did this ones profits go?

"Been married long sir?" he asked by way of an opener

"Two years Inspector"

"Seems an intelligent lady and if you don't mind my saying so sir – a very beautiful one too!"

"Thank you. Can I offer you a drink or is that not admissible?"

"No thank you sir. A bit early in the day for me. Do you mind if we get down to business?"

The Inspector watched as Roberts poured himself a large malt whisky.

"It's been a frantic day. Herbert's unexpected leave of absence has caused quite a few problems."

The little man took a hard swallow before easing his thin frame behind the double sized oak-veneered desk.

Peters guessed he was around forty. It was difficult to be more accurate with the dyed hair and toupee but as with most men approaching middle age, the sunken dissipation of the eyes was a good indicator. A passing thought occurred to him that he might be better off without the younger Candy but this type of person liked to be admired for his expensive trappings. It was the narcissism of the Accountancy profession. Boring job but with fast cars and pretty women as compensation.

Peters waited until the other man was settled. There was no hurry as far as he was concerned.

The phone rang. Roberts excused himself and answered it.

"No you've just missed her," he said, "try the boutique."

"Someone for Candy," he said on replacing the receiver. "She runs a small business of her own; brings in a few extra pennies" he smiled nervously. "Now how can I help Inspector?"

"As you know Mr Roberts, your partner's wife Mrs Joyce Mitchell is very concerned over the whereabouts of her husband and I was wondering whether you could enlighten me concerning his movements yesterday."

"Yes, yes of course. I have his appointment diary here. Unfortunately Herbert did not religiously fill it in which does make it difficult for Mrs Webb his secretary. Clients are always telephoning and she has no idea where he can be contacted. However, as you can see, he did have an appointment last evening at Compton Post Office at 8.15pm"

Peters gave the diary a cursory glance and wrote down the name Hagan in his notebook.

"Mind if I use your phone?" he gruffed.

"Go ahead"

Whilst he was waiting for a reply, Peters pulled out the packet of mints and offered one.

"No thank you Inspector – the whisky is my prop. Listen would you like me to get Mrs Webb in here for you?"

"All in good time sir. Ah Les, Peters here!" Dougie thought he could hear some tomfoolery going on in the background but even as he thought it the commotion ceased.

"I'm here at Mitchell and Roberts. Mr Mitchell had an appointment with a Mr Hagan at Compton Village Stores last evening. Get round there and check it out."

Dougie listened as the Detective Sergeant made some feeble excuses about a 'hit and run' car accident before continuing

"No Sergeant Grainger. I want you do to this one not some 'rookie' like Shone. See to it." he slammed down the telephone, annoyed with himself as much as anything.

"What was your partner like?" he demanded of Roberts.

"A good man Inspector as far as I know. He took me on as a controlling partner a year ago. Diligent, well respected and a specialist on small business. Been a qualified accountant for twenty years – loved the job and his family life, no hang-ups. What more can I say?"

"Not the sort of man to disappear without telling anyone?"

"No sir. Very level headed. If he had any worries, he did not discuss them with me!"

"Any particular client's case giving him problems?"

"No more than usual"

"How about you sir?"

"What do you mean?"

"Have you any skeletons?"

Roberts looked shocked. His face fell as if being falsely accused.

"I don't think I like the way this conversation is going Inspector but for your information – no I've nothing to hide."

Peters wasn't convinced. He thought he'd touched a raw nerve but it could wait.

"I'll have a word with his secretary now if you don't mind sir," he said with contradictory charm. "Thank you for your assistance."

****

Mitchell's secretary Jan Webb could not add anything other than Herbert often thrashed Jeremy at squash, which wasn't earth shattering news as far as he was concerned and he left the office a puzzled man. The day had not gone too kindly for him apart from the look of indignation on Robert's face when he'd jokingly asked whether he was hiding something. The accountant obviously was – but what?

Peters was now walking idly down Etherton High Street. It had ceased raining but the low clouds were bringing dusk that much earlier. He remembered suddenly that he'd given his last fiver to WPC Harrington and had no ready cash and Angela had asked him to bring some bread and milk with him on his way home from HQ. He crossed nimbly over to the bank and cursed under his breath when he found the heavy doors locked. He looked over at the Town Hall clock, which showed 4pm. Pulling out his wallet, he took a couple of paces to the cash point machine, trying desperately to remember his card's identification number. Was it 6243 or 6234? He chanced his arm and tapped out the digits. Nothing happened and the machine refused point blank to even return his plastic card.

"Well, well, well. If it isn't Inspector Peters raiding a bank!" came a voice at his shoulder. He didn't need to spin round. He recognised the distinctive Anglo/American lilt instantly but he swivelled round automatically anyway.

The grin on Gary Barker's face and the positive shake of his hand were genuine enough. Inside, Peters was pleased to see his adversary of two years previous but outwardly he tried not to show it.

"The face I recall but the name escapes me!" he said lamely.

Gary ignored him as he turned to the lorry driver who was handing down his holdall.

"Thanks very much for the lift mate" he said "much obliged."

The driver gave him a 'thumbs-up' signal before pressing hard on the accelerator.

"Had to scrounge a lift – had an accident on my way here" he continued nonchalantly. "Actually I've a lot to thank your mob for Inspector. The steering on my SAAB packed in on the motorway and I ploughed into an embankment. As you can see I escaped in one piece and the friendly 'blue-boys' arranged for my car to be towed away and even flagged down a car for me to get a lift. Couple of changes later, here I am in this town called Etherton and who's the first person I bump into but Dougie Peters. Good to see you and how come you get shifted from Main?"

"Inspector Peters to you Mister Barker!" Came the acid response.

"Ah – see you did remember my name. Do you know I believe you've put on a little weight"

"Very funny" said Peters dryly. It was true. Since he'd been here he had put on a few pounds. Less stress in the job he guessed.

"I suppose you're down here to investigate the missing accountant?"

"Mr Mitchell?"

"Yes"

"I had no idea you were the inspector in charge but I won't hold that against you" came the cheeky response. Gary secretly was pleased. Remembering the last case together, it augured well for this one.

Peters continued with his attempts to extract money from the machine but without success.

"Here step aside," said Gary and proceeded to thump the flat numeric surface with his large, granite like fists. The result was no money but at least the card was spat out onto the pavement.

"I should arrest your for vandalism!" said Peters as he stooped to pick it up.

"But you won't," said Gary confidently.

"What makes you say that?"

Gary fumbled in his leather jacket and pulled out a wad of notes. He carefully half folded a twenty pound note and flaunted it in the air. "Because you want to scrounge some money," he said. He was enjoying himself. "Honestly *Dougie*," he emphasised "its not a bribe."

Peters couldn't help but laugh. He liked the man who had brought a little cheer into a drab day.

"You win," he said resignedly.

"The serial number is GK16 698766 and it's genuine," said Gary. He was about to hand it over but then snatched it away again.

"Digs," he said. "Where's the best place for digs?"

"Come with me and I'll introduce you to Mrs Haines bed and breakfast establishment"

"And final question. Which was Mr Mitchell's favourite watering-hole?"

"Watering hole?"

"Pub!"

"According to my sources, the Compton Arms"

"Thank you Inspector," said Gary and he handed over the note. Before the officer could return with a comment, the intrepid private investigator continued as if reading his thoughts.

"Yes Inspector, I remember the last time. This time will be different and I promise to pool my information."

They began walking together up the High Street. On the opposite side of the road, the long legs and pale lemon cashmere dress of Candy Roberts rode high.

Both heads swung in the same direction. The lady did not return their lecherous stares. Gary could not help commenting

"Heh man. Nice place you've got here!"

Chapter Seven

Sgt Grainger introduced himself to the elderly man behind the Post Office counter.

"I'm looking for a Mr Hagan – Detective Sergeant Grainger," he said.

"You've found him. What can I do for you?" came the meek, almost apologetic response.

Compton Village Stores was a 'mish-mash' of a bygone era. No Retail Analyst had as yet stepped through this establishment and gained favour for streamlining it into a self-service supermarket. Here, they stocked everything from a box of matches to half a pig – with a difference. You got individual service, even if it wasn't always with a smile.

Edgar Hagan had run the store/post office with his wife all his life. He'd been tempted to change things over the years, especially during the Sixties when supermarkets had grabbed a hold and many of his regulars had deserted him for Etherton, Redditch or even Birmingham. Tempted he may have been but Edgar had stuck to his guns and true to his instinct he'd seen through the bad period. People drifted back to him once the novelty had worn off or the expense in travelling had got through to their pockets. Either way, the place still had that 'air' of post-war ration book feel to it. Now, as he was approaching retirement, it was too late to change even if he wanted to.

The portly police officer took in the ancient surrounds. Despite being a 'local' himself and frequenting the Compton

Arms barely fifty yards down the road, he rarely used the village stores. His wife did of course but if he himself required pipe tobacco, which was his main vice, he tended to buy it in Etherton. The only occasion that he would frequent the 'time-warp' was if he forgot her birthday and needed a card in a hurry. Even then, he'd been served either by a woman or a young lad.

Mr Hagan was sat behind the screen of the postal counter, which was hidden away in a corner and smothered by various pieces of post office literature, stuck with the proverbial cellotape. Much of it, he noticed, was out of date.

The only other occupant in the shop was a gangly teenage assistant who was engrossed in the sports pages of a newspaper behind the cigarette counter and who Sgt Grainger recognised as the lad who'd served him previously.

The old man continued to eye the officer suspiciously. It was rare to receive a visit from the police, let alone CID.

"Nothing to worry about sir," said Grainger noticing the concern. "Is there anywhere we can talk privately?"

Mr Hagan nodded and ushered him towards the rear of the store. Before following him he called over to the assistant.

"Paul! Mind the store – I'll be but a few minutes.

In contrast to the drab conditions out front, the kitchen into which the sergeant was guided was modern in the extreme. It boasted a wealth of electric gadgets, laminated work tops and domestic appliances. The room had obviously only recently been converted.

The elderly man saw the quizzical expression on the officer's face.

"The wife," he said as if that explained everything, "felt it was time we enjoyed the profits of the fruits of our labour."

Les Grainger smiled. Even the proprietor spoke in words of a bygone era.

"We understand sir that the accountant Mr Herbert Mitchell should have visited you last evening?" he questioned, his eyes scanning a commercial microwave oven.

"That's right. Arrived at 8 left at 9"

"Could you be a little more specific about the nature of his visit?"

Sgt Grainger was now reaching for his notebook to keep a record of the conversation and he could see a look of concern dash hurriedly across the little man's eyes.

"Has something happened to him?" he asked. The words were rushed and as a result the speech came across somewhat slurred.

"You know something don't you sir?" Les Grainger might well be slow and methodical in his police duties but he could normally tell when someone was withholding information – especially a Worcestershire local. It was always in the eyes!

"Not exactly," came the blunt response. "Only that's his son on the counter out front."

Again Grainger had to prompt him.

"Nature of Mr Mitchell's visit first if you don't mind sir"

"VAT"

"Pardon"

"Tax – bloody tax." The soft voice was now raised as if he'd been done a serious misjustice. "Apparently I registered late for this Value Added Tax thing and all of a sudden I'm being harassed by these VAT people the Revenue and accountants!"

"So Mr Mitchell was here to advise on your tax affairs?"

"That's right. Said he'd try and get the interferers off my back for a bit but I'd have to cough up some cash on account."

"Really sir"

"Yes damn them. Gave him £2,500 in cash. God knows where I'm going to get the rest from. The buggars will bleed me dry!"

"In cash sir - £2,500 in cash. Don't you have a bank account?"

"Only on the Post Office side. Had to – they insisted, otherwise they wouldn't pay me my wages for doing it"

"Did Mr Mitchell give you a receipt?"

"Oh yes! I mustn't blame him. He's a decent sort of man who's doing his best for me. Last accountant I had – bloody useless he was. He ...."

"So it was definitely £2,500 in cash?" Sgt Grainger interrupted. He wanted to make sure the old man wasn't senile about it.

"Said so didn't I. Twenties and tenners it was – broke my heart"

"Can I ask sir, if you knew Mr Mitchell was missing why you did not call the police over this money?"

"I've been thinking about it." Hagan's head lowered itself so that it was looking at the floor and he shuffled over to the refrigerator where he extracted a pint of milk before proceeding to fill a chipped beaker, which had seen better days. It looked decidedly out of place amongst the modern surroundings.

After a sip of the milk he said.

"I thought that as I had a receipt I would be covered and anyway I'm sure he'll turn up soon."

"What makes you say that?"

"Well its what his son seems to thing. Said he was a routine sort of man who wouldn't stay away for long. Perhaps he's just taken a couple of days off." Although Edgar Hagan said this, he didn't sound like a man convinced.

Les Grainger was of a more cynical nature. £2,500 was a tidy temptation.

"Did Mr Mitchell say where he was going after he left you?" he asked.

"Only that he had another client to see but he didn't say who," came the reply.

"And he left at nine?"

"Yes"

"Good. That will be all for now sir." He closed the pocket notebook and prepared to leave the kitchen. As he did so, Edgar Hagan called him back.

"Sergeant"

Les Grainer turned in his slow, ponderous manner. Hagan had that quizzical look again.

"Do you require the receipt for the money?"

"Not at this stage sire"

"Well, should the worst come to the worst and Mr Mitchell not turn up, do you think the VAT people will accept the explanation?"

"I don't know sir," he said and then added sarcastically "perhaps you'd better check with a good accountant!"

On his way out of the store, Les stopped to have a few words with Paul Mitchell. He listened carefully to the young man's account of the morning's events concerning his mother's hysterical condition but made no comment. The youth also ratified what Mr Hagan had told him concerning his father's appointment of the previous evening. Unfortunately nothing new was gleaned.

He left the shop with a hint of adventurous spirit by purchasing 2ozs of his favourite pipe tobacco and a definite feeling that whatever had happened to Mr Mitchell; somewhere along the line a serious crime had been perpetrated.

****

"Mrs Mitchell? Gary Barker hurriedly pushed the coin into the phone box situated on the bar. "Its Mr Barker here, we spoke on the phone this morning remember? Look, I've arrived in

Etherton and if it's alright with you I'll call round to see you tomorrow." He listened politely to her agitated plea for information concerning her husband but with sincerity had to honestly admit that so far he had drawn a blank. After promising to phone her the instant he heard anything, he replaced the handset and swallowed the last mouthful of lager.

"Another pint landlord," he said tapping the bar with the empty glass.

It was early evening in the Compton Arms but despite this, already there was a smattering of locals enjoying a drink.

Whilst waiting for a refill, Gary took the opportunity to survey his unfamiliar surroundings. it wasn't so much he was interested in the faded photographs of the pub's recent history or the tourists delight of discovering an olde worlde English pub. More from force of habit in the nature of detective work than the former, he quickly took in the rustic lines of both the pub and its inhabitants.

"Senor?"

Gary turned sharply back to the bar to be faced by the distinctive features of a foreign barman.

"Oh yes of course," he said searching through his pockets for some money.

"You are looking for someone no?"

"Not really. Just acquainting myself with the pub!"

"Of course senor. Are you – how do you say it – passing through?"

Gary studied the little man's features. Somehow he didn't quite fit in with the surrounds. The man looked strangely out of place in a Worcestershire pub of country folk and he imagined that he must have a hard time of it in terms of resentment from such people. Gary knew how difficult some village folk could be and looking at the workers before him, he'd be surprised if they were any different.

"You could say that," he said, counting the coins into his hands.

"Actually I'm staying here for a bit – relations in the area.

If you don't mind me saying so, its unusual to see a foreigner running an English pub in the countryside."

The man's eyes rolled to the ceiling.

"If I 'ere that once I 'ere it a thousand times," he said.

Gary was fast with the apology.

"Sorry," he said. "I didn't mean to offend. Spain is it?"

"Si"

"Are you the landlord?"

A smile broke out across his lips showing a good set of teeth, marred only by a slight chip at the bottom of one of the main canines.

"Si," he said again with obvious pride. "Senor Edwardo Stefano at your service. And if I might say it is unusual too for us to have a – how do you say 'coloured' man in our establishment?"

"Touche." Gary laughed and extended his hand.

"Barker's my name," he said, "people call me Gary"

The Spaniard seemed pleased to shake his hand. Gary thought it may well have been because he was grateful for the opportunity to talk with someone. None of the locals appeared over exuberant with the little man as far as he could tell, though one or two looked his way. The colour of his skin still made some people stare, especially in country spots.

"Edwardo," he said emphasising his name and ushering him nearer to him. "Can I talk with you privately?"

The man's eyes lit up with inquisitiveness and his chest seemed to swell with the mention of the word 'private'.

"Of course senor – that is what we landlords are here for!"

"Well the trouble is I'm here for a week and am a little short of readies"

"Readies? What is readies?"

"Dinero," said Gary, remembering his schoolboy Spanish.

"Ah si dinero." Again the landlord hovered over the bar; so much so that Gary could smell the garlic on his breath.

"I was wondering whether you are a gambling man?" Gary asked. He hoped he'd judged his character correctly. Though on the outside he looked the sort of man that would gamble there was something in his eyes and mannerisms that gave an absurd hint of sheer bravado. Gary guessed correctly that the Spaniard had lost too heavily in the past to be tempted by games of chance.

"Senor!" Again the eyes looked to the ceiling and this time the hands spread out in a gesture of defeatism.

"I used to but it is the wife you know," he said

"Pity" said Gary apparently dejected.

"However," came the immediate response. "If it is only for a few days that you are here perhaps I can help you"

"How?" said Gary, deliberately narrowing his eyes in a look of desperation.

"I could do with some 'elp behind ze bar senor"

"Terrific," that would be great." Gary needed a base to work from and as Inspector Peters had said, the Compton Arms was Herbert Mitchell's favourite watering hole, what better place to work from! Pubs made excellent information centres.

"When can I start?" he added.

"Tomorrow night 7pm"

"Your on"

The Spaniard moved away to answer the bell that was being rung by a customer in the lounge and Gary returned to his pint.

Presently the pub filled up as the 'nine to fivers' gradually drifted in to join the manual workers who by now were well oiled on the local brew. The previously quiet surrounds were now beginning to ooze with a convivial atmosphere of a cross section of community life.

By 9.30pm the place was alive and Edwardo was joined by his wife who immediately came over to Gary.

"Mister Barker?" She asked

For a moment Gary was stunned. The lady was not what he'd expected.

"Yes," he managed to say

"My husband says he's taken you on for a few days. Have you worked behind a bar before?"

"Yes," he lied. He couldn't get over the fact of how a weasel like Stephano could be married to such a Latin beauty. It wasn't just the face, though it was a face that a man could have 'wet dreams' over. Far from that. This lady had a certain gypsy quality about her. Long dark hair with tight curls that touched her delicate shoulders, handmade sweater in black with the Spanish word "Hermosa" meaning beautiful, embroidered in gold from the shoulder diagonally to the waist and the jewellery. It was the jewellery, coupled with the wild eyes that gave the gypsy look. Gold droplet earrings, gold cross around the neck, gold bracelets and gold rings on every finger! The 'jewel in the crown' of the rings that adorned her fingers was one particularly large red, fiery one on the third finger of the delicately boned right hand. This one was wicked, star-shaped and rising to a pyramid point fully three quarters of an inch above the index finger. In the artificial lantern lights hung over the bar, it appeared to mesmerise the observer like some hypnotic charm.

From his side of the bar, Gary could not see from the waist down but he imagined that such a vision would have great legs.

The expression on the woman's face did not tie in with the vision before him. The dark eyes were not 'alive' and the mascara was smudged.

The detective in him made him think that she'd recently been crying and the emotional side of his nature made him want to ask the question why. Instead all he could manage was a limp "Are you feeling okay. You look a little upset!"

"It is nothing," she said and embarrassingly added "onions from the kitchen."

"Of course," but he didn't believe her for one moment. She was hiding something and Gary wondered what!

"I just thought you might like to know the monies per hour," she said

"No matter," said Gary. "I see you have customers waiting – tomorrow will do"

She frowned but didn't respond. As she walked away to serve, Gary's eyes followed her. She did indeed have good legs encapsulated in sheer black nylon with a dainty gold bow at the ankle.

"Any chance of getting by you for a drink," said a voice at his shoulder. Gary moved politely aside to let a young lad through at the now quite congested public bar.

"Maria, when you've got a minute we're dying of thirst at this end."

Gary observed him. He decided the kid could not have been more than eighteen and by the looks of him he'd had a few drinks already. He did not want to get involved with any local who'd had too much to drink – not at this stage; he didn't want his cover blown. Besides, he was now feeling tired. It had been an eventful day with the SAAB accident, Inspector Peters and now the pub. The more he thought about it, the better the bed at Mrs Haines B&B looked. A final gulp of the local brew and he was gone, out into the night seemingly unobserved. Unobserved that is in his eye but not from the likes of Edwardo and Maria Stephano. Both pairs of eyes followed the rear of the leather coated stranger through the swing doors.

****

He thought he was dreaming. She was above him, her body arched backwards and with her hands grasping his calves. Her breasts were thrust towards his face and again his tongue worked on the excited nipples whilst his hands firmly gripped her buttocks. She was doing all the work and it was like the rise and fall of the tide on a sandy beach. It was torrid, earthy stuff and it was only when it was all over that Gary realised that the dream was reality.

As their exhausted bodies lay side by side in that Etherton guest house she spoke in that mature, sexy voice of hers.

"Now tell me you're not glad to see me!"

Gary rolled over onto his side to look at her. The room was strangely lit by a full moon peeping through a gap in the curtains and it highlighted a large freckle just below her navel. Jacky's naked body now glistened with perspiration and her normally lustrous black hair had been straightened by the efforts of her exertions.

He half smiled creating a dimple in his cheek. It was a smile, which he knew she adored.

"I thought I was dreaming," he said.

"Some dream," Jacky raised herself onto one shoulder and began running her fingers through the tight little curls on his chest.

"I had to come," she said. "Decided I could do with a holiday and thought I'd surprise you. Actually I'm being terribly naughty as I've booked a room next door but one. I didn't want to upset your Mrs Haines. I mean she's a charming enough old dear but I don't think she'd stand any impropriety under her roof!"

Gary laughed. She was right of course. Mrs Haines kept an orderly guest house and she reminded him of holiday seaside landladies when he was a child. Woe betide any couple being found together in bed if they were unmarried.

"How did you find out where I was staying?" he asked.

"Did what any good detective would have done," she stated simply.

"Checked with the local police I suppose"

"They are very helpful. I just called in and spoke to a delightful young officer and asked him for the best, and knowing you, the homeliest bed and breakfast establishment in Etherton. He was really rather dishy, I could almost have fancied him but he was a little on the young side for my taste. He said Mrs Haines at Glencoe and I called round. Had a quick look at the register and checked for your name and booked in. Simple really!"

Gary relaxed and enjoyed the experience of the softness of her touch on his chest. He was pleased she'd arrived. Apart from the physical aspect, she'd brought her Golf GTI, which would prove useful, seeing as he was without transport. He closed his heavy eyelids and within seconds he was back to sleep and this time he really was dreaming.

Chapter Eight

The fog had clamped down early again, so much so that the first wisps of smoke at 'Peaceful Waters' were undetected. By the time Etherton Fire Brigade arrived shortly after 3am, the garages were well ablaze. Firemen were still fighting desperately to save the fire spreading to the mansion as Inspector Peters and Sgt Grainger approached the scene.

They were met by Station Officer Gordon whose facial expression immediately conveyed to them, the look of a man who had failed to save a life. Words were unnecessary and the police officers dutifully followed in his footsteps, taking care not to tread on the hoses, which were pumping pressurised water onto the shell-like remains of the burning inferno.

There was plenty of activity but the three men seemed not to notice it as their feet crunched across the gravel towards a black plastic bag which lay disregarded at the edge of the manicured lawn in front of the fogbound house.

The fire officer reached the bag first, pointed to the zip and proceeded to retreat to a safe distance.

"Do the honours Sergeant," said Peters to his subordinate.

Sgt Grainger threw the inspector a filthy look. Without looking and by the length and shape of the bag, he knew instinctively what it contained.

Peters absent mindedly reached into his raincoat pocket for the familiar packet of mints and popped one into his mouth. He too knew that this was a moment of truth. Death in any shape or form still shook the organs of this onlooker and at least a mint temporarily would thwart the dryness in his mouth.

At first sight the body appeared like one of those pictures on doctor's walls where the human anatomy is shown in two contrasting vertical dimensions. The one half remained fully clothed and seemingly untouched by the fire. In contrast, the other half was nothing but pitch-blackness right down to the bone. There was no skin, muscle tissue or organs. The ferocity of the fire had melted, roasted and eventually cremated this side of the body, so that all that remained was a crinkled mass of spent matter; the result of gallons of water on a high temperature surface.

Peters thought he'd already seen enough and was in the process of turning away from the half-melted corpse when Sgt Grainger grabbed his attention.

"Look at the neck sir!" he grunted and changed position from a standing to crouched stance by the body.

The inspector followed his partner's lead and crouched alongside him. Though the suit was drenched and the man's skin glistened with droplets of water – there was no mistaking the gaping wound across the throat. The single slash travelled halfway to the ear where it tapered to no more than a scratch.

Peters studied it closely, trying hard not to let his eyes drift to the macabre side of the carcass. The wound was a positive suggestion of murder and the investigative side of his nature now came into play. What he was seeing was no longer a victim of some inexplicable, accidental tragedy but a case of suspicious death by foul play.

"Is it him?" asked Grainger quietly.

Peters directed his head towards the officer whose eyes appeared half glazed in the smoggy atmosphere.

"Yes," he said resignedly its Herbert Mitchell. Zip him back up and get the 'path' boys alerted. I'd better have a word with Gordon before we go."

As he walked the short distance towards the fire chief, Inspector Peters mind was troubled. It wasn't just the crime that bothered him but his human conscience as to how he was going to break the news to Mitchell's wife. He found such a duty was the hardest part of a policeman's job. For him bereavement of a stranger was a nightmare and he'd almost wished WPC Harrington hadn't shown him the photograph of the missing accountant.

Station Officer Gordon had remained at a discreet distance whilst the officers inspected the remains. His men now had the fire under control and he waited patiently for the inevitable police questions that would follow. A figure approached him through the soupy, grey mist clad in a dark raincoat and as it came nearer, he could see the frowning expression on the gaunt-like face of Inspector Peters. The man looked genuinely distressed.

"A bit of a mess Inspector I'm afraid," said Gordon stating the obvious. "There was nothing we could do, the body was well alight by the time we reached him."

The Inspector nodded.

"Of course, I understand," he said. Peters looked over towards the scene of the crime where four firemen were busy dousing the small pockets of flame that remained. Even from this short distance their bodies were only distinguishable by the bright yellow of helmets and leggings, their tunics merging into the blackness of the garage shrouded by fog.

"Is it safe to have a look in the garage?" he asked.

"Provided you don't mind some heat and smoke"

"Having looked at the corpse, I think I can take it," said Peters nonchalantly and together they cautiously advanced to the burnt-out building.

The heat was almost unbearable as it reflected outwards from the buckled metal of an automobile parked inside. There was, in addition to the smoke, a pungent smell from the car's melted tyres and Peters was forced to place a handkerchief to his nose and mouth. Consequently his muffled question to the Fire Officer was barely audible.

"Where did you find him?"

"Pardon"

"I said where did you discover the body?"

"Lying alongside the garage door"

Peters said nothing. A preliminary study of the blackened remains of the garage was a police textbook necessity but straight away he could tell that the fire had destroyed any obvious clue. He would have to wait for the expert forensic reports, which irritated him as he despised delays in cases of this nature.

Reluctantly due to the intense heat and smoke he rushed out of the confined space and into the 'fresh' air. Station Officer Gordon followed him and Peters was annoyed to see that the effects of the smoke and heat did not appear to have bothered him. He supposed the man was conditioned to such an occurrence but it riled him, especially when he instructed him on how to breathe once he was out.

"Feeling better Inspector?" asked Gordon after a minute or two.

Peters throat and lungs by now were sore from his spluttering and coughing experience and he was grateful for the plastic mug of water offered him.

"Smoke's a killer," the fireman continued, "it doesn't take a lot."

Peters gulped down the water and ran the back of his forearm across his eyes to remove the droplets of tears that were streaming down his cheeks.

"Foolish of me," he said, acknowledging the expert. "Tell me is there anything you think I should know?"

Gordon waited until the police officer had composed himself before answering.

"Well yes Inspector. I've something in my car which might interest you – we'll talk as we go"

Dougie listened with keen interest as the fireman explained how the body was found lying on its back adjacent to the 'up and over' doors to the garage when they arrived. The side facing him had been untouched by the flames but the side facing the rear of the building was an inferno. Naturally their first task had been to drag the man clear. The flames had been too severe to smother him with blankets – hence they'd trained the hoses on him.

By now the two men had reached the fireman's car and

Gordon firmly gripped the passenger door handle. With a flourish he tugged it open.

"This was in front of the man as we dragged him clear," he said pointing to a red hardback type accounting ledger with the word "Caledonian" emblazoned in gold upon it.

Peters reached into the pockets of his raincoat and pulled out a pair of gloves.

"Fingerprints," he said knowingly.

"Ah yes of course," said Gordon. "Fortunately my wearing of fire gloves may have helped you there!"

The book was undamaged apart from several chalk-like scratch marks across its cover where the gravel had come into contact with it during the dragging of the corpse's body. Fortunately the body had protected it from the garage blaze.

Treating it like a treasured first edition, Inspector Peters carefully opened the cover and then surprisingly had to stop himself as several sheets of smaller paper almost slid out. With patience he tucked them back in but not without noticing what they were and who they appertained to. Under the heading of The National and United Bank was the name and address of one of its customers. The pieces of paper were bank statements in the name of 'Mr E Stephano, T/as Compton Arms Public House'.

Peters closed the ledger and for the first time since arriving at the scene of the crime allowed himself a wry smile. At least he was pretty sure who Herbert Mitchell's last client was – that is the official one before his appointment with death.

****

"Well Mr Barker, as I've already said I have told all I know to the police"

"That's as maybe sir but I've travelled a long way to see you on behalf of my client Mrs Joyce Mitchell and I'm sure she would expect you as her husband's partner to be equally, if not more frank with me, than the police."

Gary crossed his legs and as he did so the friction between the seat of his trousers and the vinyl leather-look couch made a squeaking sound similar to a rude body noise. He tried not to look embarrassed and concentrated instead on the framed certificate mounted on the wall behind Jeremy Roberts shoulder. It boldly stated that Jeremy Augustus Roberts had been admitted as a member of the Association of Accountancy Technicians, followed by a large red seal and the signature of the authorising dignatory.

"Most impressive," he thought. Looking around the High Street office he quickly came to the conclusion that it was probably the only authentic fitting in the room. Even the accountant sitting opposite him looked over-gilded with his brash suit, loud tie and matching pocket handkerchief. The whole scenario reminded Gary of a well-known advertising gimmick "WOULD YOU BUY A SECOND-HAND CAR FROM THIS MAN?"

The brash suit leant forward across the desk towards him, his hands interlinked with one another like a politician about to make a party political broadcast.

"Mr Barker," he said. "Of course I too am worried about Mr Mitchell's disappearance and naturally I am concerned that Joyce is beside herself with worry." He paused and with an effort he tried to sound sincere.

"My heart goes out to her but as I told Inspector Peters the last recorded appointment in the diary was with Mr Hagan at Compton Post Office for 8.15pm. Now I'm a busy man so perhaps you'd like to pop along to his secretary's office and have a word with Mrs Webb. She'll be pleased to fill you in on any other questions concerning his clients. Good morning to you!" He rose and offered his hand, which Gary took and gripped strongly. Even the handshake felt slimy, but what was really on Gary's mind was how Herbert landed himself with such an obnoxious man as a working partner.

Mrs Jan Webb on the other hand was a delightful opposite.

She was a roly-poly, bubbly ball of fun, who was only too willing to help him and seemed excited to be given the opportunity.

"A real detective," she said showing genuine approval. "I've never met one before. I thought they only existed in the movies."

Gary laughed and subconsciously his hand reached inside his leather jacket to reassure himself the Baretta still nestled there. It was done in much the same way as a man who checks on his wallet.

"Well," he said. "I'm real and here's my business card to prove it."

She took the offered card and avidly read the words out loud. GB Private Investigations – well I never." She looked up from the card and across at the man before her. He was tall, smartly dressed but casual in black leather jacket and tight grey jeans and matching slip-on shoes. The shirt was a silky blue and open at the neck to show a tiny gold St Christopher nestling comfortably against the skin which was of a light brown colour similar to coffee. The face was clean-shaven and he had surprisingly thin lips and narrow nose. It was an honest face she decided, crowned with a top of steel-grey hair. She realised she was staring but the blue eyes seemed to hold her spellbound.

"Do I pass the audition?" asked Gary.

"Sorry," she said. It was silly. Here she was, plump and middle-aged drooling like a teenager. "As I've said I have never met a private investigator before." Laughingly she quickly added "you can investigate me anytime!"

"Cheeky"

The preliminaries over they got down to the business of going through the files of clients that Mr Mitchell dealt with. Gary was grateful that his secretary was so helpful. Within half an hour he had a break down list of all clients and their relationship with the practice. From her information and knowledge it soon became clear that Herbert Mitchell was held in high esteem and that very few had switched to other accountancy firms. On the other hand many new clients had joined the practice on recommendation and Gary could tell that the man indeed had a high workload. This was hardly surprising having met his wimp of a partner. He guessed that without Herbert the practice would undoubtedly suffer and Jan confirmed this.

"I shouldn't really be telling you this," she said, enjoying the opportunity to impart with office gossip "but quite frankly I don't know where Mr Roberts is half the time. Whenever I telephone a client's that he should be at, he's either not there or already left. Sometimes the clients aren't even expecting him in on the days that he tells me that's where he'll be. Goodness knows what he gets up to!"

"Really," said Gary mentally storing every scrap of information. "Perhaps he's got a lady friend?"

"Hadn't thought of that – you could be right of course."

"What about Mr Mitchell? Would you say he was a ladies man?"

"Good heavens no. I know Joyce very well. I think you'd be on the wrong track there."

"But marriages do go stale!" Gary offered this suggestion almost nonchalantly as he thumbed through the clients files in the office cabinet.

Jan thought about this for a moment before responding.

"I still don't believe so in this case." Seeing the detective engrossed in one of the files, she curtly added, "you will remember that confidentiality is paramount in an accountancy practice"

"Of course." Gary swung round to face her and smiled, showing a perfect top set of teeth. "Actually you'll probably be able to tell me far quicker if Mr Mitchell had any problem clients. You know the sort of thing I mean – grudges, questions concerning his professional ability, that sort of thing."

"Well of course we have a few. Every business does but now that you come to mention it, currently I can only think of one – J.C. Holdings. They recently went into liquidation and Mr Cowling the owner blamed Mr Mitchell for the collapse.

Fabrication of course but when a business does fold, people blame everyone but themselves!"

"What happened?"

"Oh all sorts of legal threats but if you look at the file you'll see that in the end Mr Mitchell clearly exonerated himself from all blame and that's the last we heard of it."

Gary took her advice and read the file. He didn't understand all of it but the crux of the matter hinged on Mr Mitchell's valuation of the stock. It appeared however, that the accountant hadn't actually been responsible, as the figure supplied was in Mr Cowling's own handwriting.

"Hoisted by his own petard!" thought Gary as he closed the file but in view of the foregoing written threats and even a newspaper article blaming his accountant for his business collapse, the detective thought it might well be worth while paying the man a visit.

"Do you know where I can contact Mr Cowling now?," he asked Jan.

"Just up the road," she said "finishes with one business and somehow or other starts up another. Runs the town's nightclub. It s called Justine's"

"Then I think I'll pay him a visit," said Gary. "Its time I stretched my legs."

He strolled leisurely away from the filing cabinet to the office door, looked back and said

"Never was much of a person for office work. I'll be back." He winked at her, smiled and eased himself out into the corridor.

Jan's eyes followed him through the glass-panelled windows as he confidently made his way towards the outer door. She couldn't help thinking that if only she were 15 years younger and two stone lighter, maybe the two of them might have had something going between them. With or without Gerald her solicitor husband finding out; she felt it would well be worth it!

Chapter Nine

Mr Jeremiah Cowling was not pleased to see Gary Barker. The last thing he wanted was a private investigator poking his nose into his business affairs. He stood with his back to the full-length two-way mirror that overlooked the dance area of the nightclub below. Being early afternoon, there was no one down there as Gary had discovered as he'd walked through the bar area on his way to the stairs that led up to his office. Naturally, he'd been escorted by Cowling's heavily built 'personal assistant', a man of few words but plenty of brawn. It was the 'heavy' who ushered him into the manager's office and who then stood with his back to the door to thwart any intention that Gary might have of leaving before being given permission to do so.

At first Gary thought the office was empty and he had a moment or two to take in the surroundings. The place had a luxurious smell to it, a mixture of leather and wood polish drawn together by the furniture and wooden panelling which covered three sides of the spacious room. There was no window but in the wooden panelling behind the Chippendale desk, which confronted him, there was another door, which was slightly ajar. Lighting was by means of a single candelabra in the centre of the office casting an unusual shadow across the grey bespeckled carpet.

"I won't ask you to take a seat Mr Barker," said the voice at right angles to him, "I've a feeling you won't be staying too long"

The detective turned slowly towards the owner of Justine's. He assumed it was the man Cowling by the embroidered gold initials on the breast pocket of his navy blue blazer, which like the rest of his clothing had obviously been tailored to fit. The man was short – real short. Gary decided Cowling would have difficulty making 5ft in his stockinged feet but he'd tried to compensate for this with 'lifts' in his grey Cuban heeled boots which naturally matched his trousers. Under the jacket, he wore a thin grey polo neck sweater, which was tucked into the trousers and held in place by a thin white leather belt. There were two other striking things about this short man. First he was 'aborigine' black and secondly he was bald.

"Mr Cowling I presume," Gary stated blandly.

"State your business," said the other man eyeing him up. "I'm a busy man." Still he remained with his back to the mirror.

"It concerns Mr Herbert Mitchell. I believe he used to be your accountant?"

"So"

"Well he appears to have disappeared and I've been hired to find him"

"Really"

"I'd appreciate any information you could give me"

Only now did the man shift his position and move over to the desk where he opened a box and took out a thick Havana cigar. His eyes however never left Gary for a second and he could feel them boring into him like a drill into a brick wall. Every orchestrated move that Cowling made was designed to compensate for his small stature and make his visitor feel ill at ease. Gary however remained unmoved. He could play the waiting game too.

The man lit the cigar from a gold table lighter and proceeded to blow smoke rings. When he spoke, it was more a statement than any attempt at conversation.

"Mr Barker," he said. "I have nothing to say to you. I dislike 'muck-rakers' which is how I refer to people of your so called occupation and I suggest you leave now, whilst you still have the means to do so"

"Are you threatening me?"

Cowling shrugged his shoulders and merely blew another smoke ring. Gary tried another tack.

"Isn't it true that you blamed Mr Mitchell for the failure of J.C. Holdings?"

The bald head nodded and for a fraction of a second, Gary thought the man was going to answer but it was merely the signal for the 'heavy' to act. He turned round and to one side with just sufficient speed to escape the full power of a left jab to the eye. Even so he felt the knuckle scrape the side of his temple above the ear. Gary counter-acted with a left stomach punch, which temporarily winded the big guy and followed it up with a controlled rabbit punch to the back of the neck. The man fell and as he did so his head hit the corner of the oak desk and the body crashed to the floor like a sack of potatoes. Spots of blood blotched the grey texture of the carpet but the man did not rise again.

The detective reached across the table and grabbed the lapels of Cowling's jacket and lifted the guy off his feet and across the table towards him. Keeping him firmly grasped in his left hand, Gary pulled out the Baretta from his shoulder holster and thrust the tip of the barrel under the frightened man's chin.

"Now listen to me short-arse," he said. "I've tried the polite approach but this is obviously the only language you know so talk before I really lose my temper."

It was at that moment that the door in the panelling behind the two men opened fully and a young police officer stood there in uniform. Gary caught sight of him and quickly returned the Baretta to its holster and released Cowling, who slumped back into the confines of the leather desk chair.

"A little disagreement officer – no more. I am sure Mr Cowling is prepared to talk to me now, aren't you sir?"

"What's going on and who the devil are you?" asked the police officer treading warily into the room. It was then that he saw the crumpled figure of Gary's assailant lying on the floor and he dashed over to help him. "What happened Mr Cowling?" he said looking up from the prone figure.

Cowling looked at Barker. The eyes did not appear so

menacing now – they appeared nervous as indicated by a slight twitch.

"A-an accident officer," he managed to say, "I forgot that you were still here."

Gary wasn't sure what was going on but decided to play it by ear. The 'heavy' stirred and the officer helped him to his feet. Blood was trickling from the man's ear but he appeared not to notice in his groggy state. The policeman guided him to a chair, gave him a handkerchief and said

"I'll whip you down to casualty for an X-ray in a moment sir – but you!," his voice changed from one of sympathy to discipline as he turned on Gary "had better explain fast what you're doing here."

Gary stared at Cowling looking for a lead. The man regained his composure now and took control.

"PC Almond say hello to Mr Barker – a man in not too dissimilar an occupation from yourself. He's a private detective."

Did Gary imagine it or did he see a look of mean distrust between the two coloured men and if so was it geared to each other or towards him.

"We had a little disagreement," Cowling continued, "a private matter. Perhaps you'd be good enough to leave us now and take Bert my doorman to the hospital."

Gary could see a look of bewilderment crossing the young policeman's brow. He could understand the man's predicament. If there had been a fight, it had been on private property and both partners obviously did not want to prefer charges so how was he to report this to his superiors.

As if reading Gary's thoughts the officer said.

"It's a question of my report ....."

Cowling reached for the half smoked cigar that had fallen onto the desk during the skirmish and proceeded to re-ignite it by several long draws on the butt.

"Just put in the report what you came here to do lad – that is crime prevention, checking on my windows and alarms," he said and then added with emphasis "nothing else."

When the two men had left, Cowling beckoned to Gary to take a seat. His attitude had now changed to one of civility and politeness, even to the extent of offering him a cigar, which Gary declined.

"I like a man with spunk," he said, throwing himself back into the folds of leather comfort. "Because of that and on this occasion only, I'm going to answer your questions. Whether the answers will be honest or not is for you to decide Mr Barker."

He paused before continuing.

"I know that Mr Mitchell is a diligent man, liked and respected within this community. Of course I have heard he is missing and I hope he has not come to serious harm. I've no doubt you've checked with his practice and discovered that I blamed him for the failure of my previous business. This is true and I still intend to sue, as I believe there was incompetence within the framework of the professional advice I was given. It is not only I who am dissatisfied with the services of Mr Mitchell and Roberts. My close associate Patrick Wainwright of Enterprise Transport is continually complaining about the firm, saying they are inefficient and if you'd like to check with him I believe you'll find he intends to change accountants. So you see Mr Barker I am not the only one with problems concerning that firm."

"I never said you were," said Gary dryly "you could have saved yourself and your doorman a lot of trouble by giving me this information when I first arrived."

"Ah," said Cowling as his face broke into a crooked smile, "but that wouldn't have been half as much fun. Now I think our business is concluded don't you?"

"For now," said Gary and he rose from the chair and made for the door. As he reached it, the cultured tones of Cowling made him spin round.

"Remember," he said and the menacing look returned. "That was a one-off conversation on account of the way you conducted yourself. I've now got the measure of you. Next time and I would respectfully suggest that there isn't a next time, you'll need more than reflexes and a poxy little Baretta. Good day Mister Barker!"

"Don't you worry Mr Cowling – next time and there will be a next time I'm sure – you'll need more than a 'flake' to protect your short arse. You'll need a ruddy miracle!"

Gary slammed the door behind him on the way out. He didn't know how Cowling fitted into the shape of his investigation but he had a feeling that somewhere along the way the man was in it, right up to his scrawny little neck!

Chapter Ten

"Can I help you?"

Gary stood there confused. For a moment he thought he'd entered the wrong office but there was no mistaking the occupant. It was the lady that he and Inspector Peters had admired from across the High Street the previous day.

"Eh – sorry. I was looking for Mrs Webb" he said somewhat embarrassed by his predicament.

The woman stood up from behind the desk. As she did so, she raised a hand to gently tease her flowing blonde hair behind an ear. Continuing with the brushing stroke, she stepped forward towards him.

"Its Mrs Webbs afternoon off," she said smiling. "I'm Candy Roberts and you must be – let me guess – Mr Barker Private Investigator?"

Her model-like face broke into a welcoming smile and the hand now moved gracefully from her hair to the hip, where it slid effortlessly down the thigh of an expensive looking silk dress, as if smoothing out the creases. It was, Gary thought, a gesture of a confident woman and in body language terms it had the desired effect. His eyes automatically lowered to the stockinged legs before travelling upwards, taking in every last curve of her ripe body.

"Right," he said trying to appear cool. Inside he knew that the single word had been delivered in a croaking voice and he quickly added, "it was really Mrs Webb I came to see." He turned as if to leave but she called him back.

"Mr Barker. I'm sure if you give me the opportunity I could help. My husband Jeremy is a partner in the practice you know and I'm well versed in the firm's history"

Gary made a gesture of scratching his neck as if deciding

whether to discuss the matter with her. He wanted to be sure that Mrs Webb had put Mrs Roberts fully in the picture before discussing it further. Turning slowly to face her he said

"I'm sure you are Mrs Roberts but ...."

"Do call me Candy," she interrupted. Again the smile was warm, only this time her eyes danced outrageously. If it wasn't for Jacky, Gary thought he might easily be tempted.

"Well *Candy*," he emphasised her name. "I've been to see a Mr Cowling. I am as you are probably aware, trying to trace Mr Herbert Mitchell ....."

"And you visited Mr Cowling because the two of them fell out over his business liquidation," she finished his sentence for him.

"Yes"

"And was he any help?" she asked.

"That's just the point and why I've returned to your offices. He mentioned a Mr Patrick Wainwright and I was hoping Mrs Webb might be able to give me some background information on him. According to Mr Cowling, this man also was a little uncomplimentary about the firm."

It was Candy's turn to show a clean pair of stiletto heels. Gary couldn't help thinking how impractical such shoes were in a working capacity but he followed the long legs anyway. At the filing cabinet, she pulled out a drawer and positioned herself sideways to him so that he could see the thrust of her breast through the thin material. She was teasing him, that he knew – but why?

"Enterprise Transport," she said, pulling out a buff folder. "He's the Managing Director of a fairly small fruit and vegetable operation on the outskirts of Etherton. There's nothing in here to indicate that Mr Wainwright was dissatisfied with our services however. Quite the contrary. In fact there's a copy of a letter here from Mr Mitchell confirming an appointment for today and its worded in a most friendly manner. In view of the circumstances I would imagine Jeremy will now be handling this client but if there had been a problem, I'm sure I would have heard about it. We are a small practice Mr Barker and any problems – well my husband does confide in me you know"

"Yes of course," said Gary, "but you'll appreciate I have to check all angles. Mrs Mitchell is in quite a state over the disappearance of her husband and it's my job to be thorough."

"And I'm sure you are," she said. Again there was a sexual hint in the way that she spoke.

"I wonder if you'd be good enough Mrs Roberts to give me Mr Wainwright's address and phone number"

"Candy," she reprimanded.

"Yes of course – Candy," he said.

"I'll write it down for you. Tell me what is your Christian name?"

"Gary"

"G-a-ary," she repeated out loud and her rose-red lips pouted as she said his name.

"I like it," she said purringly. "It suits you. Tell me G-a-ry, have you managed to discover anything of significance about poor Mr Mitchell?"

"A little," he said, "but it's not for public consumption."

"Oh," Candy's eyebrows lifted sharply and her face begat an expression of shock.

"We do know how to treat confidential information here Gary and we have been open with you. Surely you could find it in your heart to be friendly towards me. I promise it wouldn't go past these four walls."

Gary was tempted. The lady was giving him all the 'come-on' signals and Jacky was away in Cheltenham visiting 'old friends' as she put it.

"I'd like to," he said, "but I'm sorry. It would be unethical"

For the first time the lady's attitude changed to one of cool indifference as she hastily thrust the folder back into the cabinet.

"In that case," she said in a huff, "I don't think I can be of any more assistance."

Her gestures matched her mannerism as she strode quickly past him to the door, which she then flung open.

"Good day Mister Barker," she said in a voice that indicated that her previous helpfulness had been more than he deserved.

Gary shrugged his shoulders and followed her suggestion that he should leave. Determined to have the last word he said

"Its nothing personal – you do understand!" This was given with a side twist of the head and a subtle wink but it had no effect. The lady was not for turning and his wink was met with a cold, icy stare.

He continued to walk down the narrow corridor for a few seconds before inspiration made him double back. The lady was already holding what appeared to be a heated discussion over the telephone. What Gary would have liked to know was to whom she was talking!

****

It was Mrs Haines herself who greeted Gary when he returned to his accommodation. The detective was hoping he could grab a couple of hours sleep before doing his first stint behind the bar at the Compton Arms. Although he knew he shouldn't feel guilty about Jacky's deception and their impropriety of the previous night – he did so nonetheless and tried hard to avert his gaze directly from her searching eyes.

"Your evening paper Mr Barker," she called after him, as he was about to climb the stairs. "You remember you asked me to get you one for all the time you were staying"

"Ah yes – thank you Mrs Haines, that's extremely kind of you."

"No bother," she said. "Is your room alright?"

"Fine." He took the paper from her and attempted again to escape her.

"Just one moment please," she ordered.

"Here it comes," he thought to himself. "The riot act

concerning his behaviour under her roof." He nervously turned to face the imposing presence of his elderly landlady.

"The cleaner found this on the floor in your room this morning. Is it yours?"

At arms length she held out what looked like a silver curtain ring. Gary moved closer to get a better look.

"I know they're all the fashion," she continued, "but I did not notice you wearing it when you arrived."

Gary grasped her intended meaning. Of course, a lot of men wore an earring nowadays.

"Y-es. Thank you Mrs Haines. I do occasionally wear one in the evenings. I wondered where I'd misplaced it."

The woman smiled at him and he felt embarrassed. Hurriedly he took it off her and impatiently bounded up the stairs two at a time, before she had further cause to delay him further.

On reaching the safety of his room, he threw the paper onto the bed and instantly picked it up again as the headline caught his eye.

"A CORPSE IN THE VALE," it read and then in smaller print "Mystery surrounds death of local accountant."

Without bothering to read the report, he dashed back downstairs and grabbed the receiver of the hall's telephone call box. After a few moments he was connected to Etherton Police Station and breathlessly he said

"Connect me with Inspector Peters – tell him its Gary Barker!"

There was a pause before Peters answered.

"Dougie – I've just seen the papers. What can you tell me?"

"Waiting for the path report of course, but the body is definitely that of Herbert Mitchell"

"How did he die?"

"Didn't you read the newspaper report?"

"No. I don't trust newspaper stories that involve serious crime. I've seen the headlines – nothing else."

"Can't say for certain but he was badly burned in a fire and his throat appeared to have been slashed. I'm now treating it as a murder enquiry."

"Any clues?"

"Maybe. We found a set of accountancy books on him. I can't say more at this stage. We're having them checked out."

"Who's name is on the books?"

"You know I cannot give you that. Its privileged information"

"I thought we'd agreed to pool information Inspector"

There was a discreet silence at the other end.

"Inspector. I asked whose name the books were in!"

"I'm sorry Barker. Its confidential"

"In that case," said Gary heatedly, "I consider our agreement declared null and void"

He slammed the phone down angrily. "Damn the man, why did he have to be so bloody contradictory?"

Returning to his room he flopped onto the bed and despite the frustrations, surprisingly sleep came easily to him – even though it consisted mainly of mixed dreams concerning several leading Etherton characters – all of them now potential suspects for murder!

Chapter Eleven

The gangly youth appeared nervous as he approached the bar and Gary was wondering whether he should serve him a drink should he ask for it. The kid did not look eighteen but at least he was sober which did not appear to be the case the last time he'd seen him the previous evening.

"Is your name Mr Barker?" the kid asked.

Gary finished polishing the beer glass he was working on, taking care to ensure there were no smears remaining. The instructions from Senor Stefano had been that his wife was most particular about clean glasses and this being his first night behind the bar of the Compton Arms, he wanted to make a good impression.

The kid did not look much of a threat, not with that mop of blonde hair obscuring on eye and a half-circle of acne around the mouth but one never knew in his line of business.

"Who's asking?"

"Then you are Mr Barker!" The fact was now stated not questioned and Gary smiled. The kid was brighter than he had given him credit for.

"Yes I'm Gary Barker."

The youth's eyes widened to give an expression that he'd known all along that this was the private detective before him.

"Thought so," he said and then the expression vanished as quickly as it came, to its former doleful look.

"I'm Paul Mitchell. You'll have heard about my father!"

"Yes – look I'm sorry – really I am"

It was now Gary's turn to express sincerity with the eyes.

"That's okay. Its hit me hard but its Mum who's really suffering. She described you to me. I hope you won't mind me saying this but we don't have too many of your sort in this part of the country."

Gary said nothing. He was already aware from the raised eyebrows of the locals, that the colour of his skin was already a talking point.

"As I was saying," Paul continued "she's taking my father's death badly but asked me to give you a message that she would like you to continue your investigation to find out the facts concerning his death"

"Has your mother got someone with her?" Gary asked, aware of the effect a bereavement can cause.

"Yes. Mrs Webb my father's secretary"

"I know her. She's a good woman. Thank you for the message Paul, I'll do all I can."

"Will yer stop yer yapping and let's have some service at this end of the bar" came a voice in the local brogue from Gary's rear. He turned to leave Paul and serve the irate customer but the youth called him back.

"I want to help," he said

"Hang on a minute"

Gary moved lithely down to the far end of the public bar where he quickly pulled a pint of draught bitter and cashed-up in the till. Fortunately, being a Wednesday, the pub was still quiet; most of the customers not getting paid until nearer the weekend.

"You were saying you want to help," he said on his return.

"Yes"

"Tell me what do you know about Mrs Roberts, your father's partner's wife?"

Paul leant further over the bar towards the detective. He dropped the level of his voice but sounded excited.

"Do you think she's involved?" he asked

"I've no idea. All I'm asking is your opinion of her and if you are to assist me young man – everything between us is in strictest confidence. Understand?"

"Yes of course. Well I don't know if it helps but I'm pretty sure she's got something going with another man. I nip over here from the Post Office shop at lunchtime for a half of lager and ….."

"You are eighteen then?" Gary interrupted

Paul looked hurt at this affront to his coming of age three weeks previous.

"Of course," he said indignantly.

"As my assistant then, I'll buy you a pint. Go-on," said Gary, "I'm listening." He poured a pint of Brennards Continental lager, cursing under his breath as the pump gushed out froth instead of amber fluid.

"She's often been here with him in the past and in fact was with him yesterday. He must be something to do with Enterprise Transport because I've seen him in one of their lorries. I can't be sure they're having an affair or anything like that but they certainly appear very friendly"

"And what did this man look like?"

"Big powerful man. Head twice the size of yours. Loud mouth, scruffy hair, in his late thirties. Wears a black bomber jacket and jeans."

"Mm," said Gary, finally managing to squeeze a full pint of lager which he unceremoniously dumped in front of Paul. "That could prove useful. Look I shall be working here nights – so pop in to see me and I'll let you know what's going on. When you return to your mother, tell her I'm still working on her case but don't let on that your helping. Understand?"

"Right Mr Barker"

"Call me Gary"

"You got it – Gary" came the response in the latest fashionable vernacular.

"Good. Look you'll have to excuse me now. Got to find out how to change a barrel."

Gary walked through the kitchen area into a small hallway and stood at the bottom of the steep staircase.

"Excuse me," he shouted upwards, "the lager's finished. Need a new barrel!"

"Coming," came a feint feminine voice from the overhead accommodation area. This was followed by a scurry of activity across the landing, ending in Gary's face to face confrontation with Cordobes. The Alsatian stood menacingly at the top of the stairs, daring the trespasser to take a pace on the bottom rung toward it. Gary kept his distance; he had no desire to get involved with the pub's guard dog which he'd heard would attack without warning anyone foolish enough to climb the staircase who did not have permission from its owners.

Moments later Maria came into view. She made a point of stroking Cordobes, who in turn raised itself on its hind legs to give her a slobbering kiss.

"That'll do," she gently admonished, "stay!" Seeing Gary waiting at the bottom she shouted, "catch" and threw down a set of keys.

"You know where the cellar is," she said. "I'll be with you in a moment."

"What about the bar?" Asked Gary. "You'll need someone to man it"

"Get that lazy husband of mine to stand in for you. You'll probably find him in the lounge!"

Mr Stephano was a little put out by the rude interruption. It appeared he'd found a new arrival on which to test his English but on hearing the instructions came from his wife, he instantly excused himself from a relieved customer.

"You see," he said, "they canna run dis a place without me – not for two minutes"

It was unusual to refer to the separate building that housed the stock as "the cellar." For one thing it was a good fifty yards from the nearest bar in the pub.

Most pubs of this age, circa 17th century, had their cellars beneath the bar area. Although there was space underneath the Compton Arms, it had not been used for fifty years or more. According to the landlady the reason for this was the dampness and possibility of flooding from the nearby river.

Gary thought this comment strange, as the pub itself was on high ground and situated a good distance from the River Avon but he did not think the subject was worth pursuing and had only mentioned the fact as a means of getting the 'gypsy' woman to be more open about herself.

"Doesn't the distance from this building to the pub cause you problems?" he asked, as Maria instructed him on how to change the heads on the pressurised beer containers.

"In the summer yes. The beer lines travel underneath the car park and on hot days this means that our Brennards Original Bitter quickly goes off. We don't sell enough of it so in the really warm weather, we don't even put a barrel on."

As she clamped down the fitting onto a new 22 gallon barrel of lager, Gary couldn't help but think that tonight her mood was one of irritability. Although she was explaining to him the rudimentaries of changing barrels, it was done in a perfunctory way and the dynamic appearance of their first meeting, by appearance at any rate, did not add up.

To begin with the long black curly hair had been swept back behind the ears and was held in place by a red ribbon above the forehead. This gave a hard look to the Latin features and the wild eyes now looked sad without the benefit of eyebrow liner or mascara. The clothes too had changed into a simple 'angora-like' sweater and old faded jeans. Only the jewellery remained constant with an abundance of gold bracelets and rings, highlighted by the spectacular fiery red stone on the third finger of her hand.

He wondered what was running through her mind. This was only the second occasion that they'd exchanged words. Previously she'd been crying – now she appeared edgy. He tried to imagine what she'd look like if only she would smile.

Maria continued with her sales pitch in a nonchalant manner.

"Each line," she said, pointing to the gauges attached to the whitewashed walls, "is indicated by the plastic barrel caps pinned to the wall." Gary followed her pointed directions. He had to concede that only an imbecile could connect the wrong tap to a barrel. Each line of product beer was clearly marked for the eight different types of draught beer available to the customer.

"Over here we have our bottle store." Her arms swept in an arc to the corner of the large refrigerated room where stacks of plastic crates containing bottled beers and minerals stood. "Only take in one crate as, and when required," she stated. "Any questions?"

"What about the locked door by the Brennards Mild?" he asked. "Do I need to know about that?"

There was a slight pause.

"Oh yes," she said. "Edwardo keeps the spirits and crisps in there. You'll have to see him about those!"

Again doubt crossed Gary's mind. If there were spirits kept there, how come he'd see Mr Stephano bring a fresh gallon bottle of whisky downstairs early in the evening when he'd first arrived for bar duty.

As if anticipating such a question and noticing Gary's frown, Maria added

"We do however keep one or two of the more popular lines upstairs."

****

The evening seemed to fly by. Gary was kept busy with serving the customers, both in the public and lounge bars. To begin with he found it difficult to work out the prices in his head and remembering to tilt the glass at a 45 degree angle when serving draught and bottled beers. This ensured that the customer obtained a good head on his beer without getting half a glass of froth.

Despite the speed with which time passed, he wasn't sorry when Mr Stephano shook the hand bell denoting 'time'. His feet were swimming in sweat from the mileage covered behind the bar and his mind was scrambled by the efforts of an evening's mental arithmetic.

"Does it get any easier?" he asked. The customers had finally gone, the washing up was completed and he sat on top of the bar allowing his aching feet to swing freely above an ice-cooled bottle shelf.

Maria poured him a half pint glass of lager.

"Here," she said ," you deserve it." She poured herself a large Martini, added ice and topped it with lemonade.

"Yes," she said, "you'll get used to it."

Gary took a good swallow of the lager. It was cool and refreshing.

"Good stuff this Brennards Continental," she said. "I've never come across it before."

"It comes from a small brewery in Cornwall near Falmouth. I believe we're the only outlet in the West Midlands area. Glad you like it."

Again Gary thought the lady was restrained. It was difficult to keep a conversation going with her and yet he felt that given the right circumstances, she could be most pleasant company. He tried a different tack.

"Where's Mister Stephano?"

"Oh, he'll be upstairs doing the books. Likes to cash-up before going to bed. Accounts for every last penny, so god help you if your not honest." She looked at him for once straight in the eye before adding "but I can see that you are."

The mention of books reminded Gary of his purpose for being behind the bar.

"Did you read about that accountant in the local paper?" he asked.

"Yes," she barely whispered, her eyes looking down at the beer-stained linoleum. "Nasty business!"

"I understand he was a regular here"

"Yes he was. Look if you don't mind, its been a tiring day ....."

"Of course. I was forgetting what a long day publicans' have. Come to think of it I'm tired too. Sorry – I hope you don't think I was being nosey"

She smiled for once.

"No of course not. It's just that I have a lot on my mind"

"I'll say goodnight then"

She saw him to the door and he heard the bolts slide home as he pulled on his anorak. Seconds later the lights were switched off, plunging the pub and car park into darkness. Gingerly he stepped out onto the pavement and headed for a distant streetlight, which barely glowed through the thick fog, which had mysteriously re-appeared since his earlier arrival at the pub.

Without realising it, he found himself in the gutter of the roadway, his eyes desperately trying to adjust to the lack of light. He heard a car in the distance coming towards him. Only when it was almost upon him did he see its headlights through the fog. Instinct saved him but only just, as he flung himself to the right towards the pavement. He felt as though he'd been sandwiched as the car hit him a glancing blow on the left shoulder; the momentum of which forced him into a solid concrete block on his right. He was spun round, losing his balance in the process and landed on his rear.

The car screeched to a halt further up the road and for a moment all was still. Gary hauled himself up and vigorously rubbed both bruised shoulders. He was about to take a step forward toward the flowing brake lights of the offending vehicle when he heard a crack and automatically he dived to the pavement. He reached for where his Baretta should have been and then remembered his holster and weapon were back in his room. Quickly he re-adjusted his hand movement to his right calf for the reserve pistol but by now the car was on the move again disappearing into the fog.

He lay still for a few seconds listening to the fading sounds of the departing vehicle before hauling himself up again. At the lamppost into which his shoulder had been forced, his fingers searched.

Someone in the pub switched the lights on and Gary could now hear the barking of Cordobes. The tips of his nails dug frantically into the chipped crevice of the concrete. With his other hand he reached into the pocket of his anorak for the penknife. He continued to gouge inside using the blade, until the tip of the bullet dropped neatly into his hand. Only then did he retrace his steps and head toward the distant fogbound streetlight, taking extra care this time not to walk too close to the kerb.

Chapter Twelve

"It says murder in the newspapers – you said it would read suicide!"

"That's something I *don't* understand – something must have gone wrong"

"Too right something's gone wrong," came the voice crackling down the line. Things are getting too hot. I want a final shipment and then a shutdown on operations. Arrange it. On completion you contact me – we're getting out!"

There was a 'click' and the line went dead. The person who had made the long distance call to London did not loiter. Seconds later, the old fashioned red telephone box situated outside the Compton Arms, was once again available for any member of the public who chose to use it.

****

Gary Barker too had his problems. It was only the second time since he'd returned from the States that someone had taken a shot at him. On the previous occasion he'd received a flesh wound in the arm but at least he'd seen it coming and had expected something of the sort. This time he had no idea of the identity of the attacker, or the reason for it. Could it be connected with this case or did it have something to do with the 'accident' on the motorway with his SAAB? A call to the garage earlier in the morning had not alleviated his fears. The mechanic couldn't be sure so he'd forwarded the suspect track-rod to the manufacturers' for analysis.

Reluctant as he was to contact Inspector Peters after his

uncooperative attitude regarding the books found on Mitchell's body, he knew it was the sensible thing to do. Surprisingly the policeman seemed to have had a change of heart and apart from his immediate promise to get 'ballistics' to check on the bullet, which Gary gave him; he even apologised for his telephone behaviour of the previous day. Peters had informed him that there appeared to be little of use in the books and that they related to the Stephano's public house. He'd had them checked for prints before passing them on to Jeremy Roberts who would investigate the figures. In the meantime he was sending Sgt Grainger around to interview the Stephanos' who had confirmed on the phone that Mr Mitchell had visited them late on the night of his disappearance.

Gary for his own part had informed the inspector that Mrs Mitchell still wished him to investigate and coincidentally he had made the Compton Arms his base under the guise of a barman. Peters agreed not to break his cover provided Gary kept him informed on any developments.

It was with these thoughts in mind that he left the confines of Etherton police station to be 'tooted' by a white Golf GTI. Jacky was back from Cheltenham and was he glad to see her!

She greeted him with a long lingering kiss as he climbed into the passenger seat and when their lips parted, breathlessly said

"Is it back to Mrs Haines for a 'quickie'?"

He looked at her expectant face, the eyes wide with flirtatious lust and the lips moist and inviting, daring him to refuse. If it hadn't been for the shooting last night, he'd have been more than eager but given the new evidence, he wanted to crack-on with the case.

"Later," he said, "we've work to do"

"Really. How exciting – where are we going?"

"To a company called Enterprise Transport. I'll navigate, you drive. Step on it!"

"Yes sir oh master! Hang on to your piece – we're gone!"

Wheels spinning, rubber burning, Gary was thrust back into his seat as she practised her Grand Prix start. It was a half-a-minute later that he found the heart to tell her she was travelling in the wrong direction!

****

Paul Mitchell's description of Wainwright had been most apt. The man had all the subtlety of a sumo wrestler and wasn't far short in weight and size of at least matching the basic requirements. His facial expression in itself looked sinister as Gary introduced himself.

"So you're a private eye – what's that got to do with me?" he demanded, handing his secretary several cheques and virtually ignoring him.

"Susie, get these into the bank straight away love before that damn manager starts bouncing our own payments."

The girl seemed relieved at having the opportunity to escape the office and as Gary looked around the room, he could understand why. Enterprise Transport was a tatty operation and no mistake. Paint peeling off the drab grey walls, paper strewn everywhere, grease sodden carpets and by the feel of the place – no heating. One didn't need to be a genius to determine that this company was sliding downhill fast.

Wainwright too was aware of the detective's searching instincts.

"You should have seen it before we started to make money," he gruffed.

"Of course," said Gary nonchalantly, "business is business – I understand. I won't take up much of your time but a close associate of yours, a Mr Cowling, referred me to you. You do know him?"

The sunken eyes narrowed.

"Sure I know Jeremiah," he said suspiciously. "What's this all about?"

"You appear to have something in common. Apparently

neither of you is to happy with your accountants Mitchell and Roberts?"

"So that's it. My accountant gets bumped off and you think I had something to do with it. Mister you're barking up the wrong tree!"

"I didn't say that"

"You implied it – same difference"

The man began searching in his desk drawers for a packet of cigarettes, found one and lit it. With a big display of machoism he took a deep inhalation and then blew the smoke out through his nostrils.

Gary studied him. An inner sense told him that like Mr Cowling, this 'overgrown ape' was up to his bull-neck in something shady. He tried a new angle.

"What's your relationship with Mrs Candy Roberts?"

The eyes now glared daggers at him.

"I don't know what you mean"

"I understand you've been seen together on more than one occasion." Wainwright made a move from the desk towards him.

"You'd better be careful what your implying 'dickhead'. Listen and listen good, if you don't want to become part of that wall. I don't take shit like that from no-one – least of all a half-breed runt like you"

Gary stood his ground. Big as the man was, his threats did not intimidate him.

"I'm not implying anything Mr Wainwright, though judging by your reaction I must say your giving me good reason to think otherwise."

"Get out Barker," the man roared, "out do you hear me?" The blood had rushed to Wainwright's face of an animal about to lose control. The detective remained calm.

"I'm sure we'll meet again," he said, keeping the man in view as he back tracked towards the door. "I'll see myself out."

He'd just made good his exit when something smashed through the glass frame of the door and whistled by him. It was only then that Gary sprinted fast across the transport yard and to the other side of the main road to where Jacky sat patiently waiting in the car.

"Do I step on it again boss?" she said as he fought to regain his breath in the passenger seat. "I take it you were made welcome by your friend Mr Wainwright?"

"Ha bloody ha"

Jacky let out the clutch and the car began to move. Gary turned to look out of the rear window. As he did so he noticed a lorry pull out from the yard and turn in the opposite direction. The rear of the lorry was laden with beer barrels, which set him thinking.

"Quick love," he said. "A 'U' turn and follow that lorry"

"I can't she said "there's too much traffic."

"Do it woman – they'll get out of the way"

The urgency in his voice captivated her and she pulled hard round on the wheel. A car travelling in the opposite direction braked, beeped its horn and flashed its lights but they made it, mounting the pavement in the process.

"Good girl," said Gary.

"What's it all about?" she asked excitedly.

"Tell me if I'm wrong but don't beer barrels travel between pubs and breweries. If so, what are they doing in a crummy transport depot?"

She looked across at him as if he was mad.

"That *is* a long shot," she said.

"It's all I've got, so do as your told and follow."

The driver appeared to be in no hurry and they had little difficulty following him through Etherton to the Compton Arms pub where they watched the unloading of what appeared to be six empty barrels. At least Gary assumed they were empty, by the way that both the driver and Mr Stephano easily managed to carry them to the cellar building. Nothing further untoward occurred and they made their way back to their B & B accommodation.

Soon after their return, Gary was called down to the hall phone box by Mrs Haines, where he was surprised to hear the voice of Jeremy Roberts.

"Inspector Peters gave me your number and asked me to keep you informed over the books found by Mr Mitchell's body," he said. His voice sounded as though he was doing Gary the biggest of favours and Gary wondered what sort of conversation had passed between the policeman and accountant. The man sounded almost reasonable.

"Its good of you to take the trouble," he offered in return.

"No trouble Mr Barker but little to tell. The pub's books appear to be fairly straightforward. The turnover is much as I would expect for one of its size, even if it's a little understated and the Gross Profit as it stands would not satisfy the Inland Revenue."

"What does that mean in English?"

"It means that Mr Stephano has taken monies out of his business. All we will do is add an amount back in order to increase the turnover and thereby profitability – to a percentage that we know the Revenue will accept. This extra money is then shown as drawings by the licensee.

"Is that normal?"

"In the public house trade yes. Pub people see so much cash going through their fingers that they think they can get away with it but we always see the signs and add it back in so that if there is tax to pay, they get caught for it."

"So there is nothing unusual about these books Mr Roberts?"

"Not in my professional opinion"

"Well I'm much obliged – thank you"

Gary replaced the receiver. The plot was thickening. An accountant had been murdered and a set of pub's books had been found alongside the body, apparently in order. A transport firm delivered empty barrels to that same pub for no apparent reason. There had to be a link between the two. He knew that his next move must be to check on the barrels in the cellar!

The opportunity came that evening in his stint behind the bar. The pub was extremely busy. Even Dougie Peters and his wife Angela were there, but true to his word he didn't let on that he had recognised Gary. Jacky arrived shortly after and Gary directed her over to where the inspector and his wife were sitting. Within minutes, from his vantage point behind the bar, Gary could see that the three of them were having a good old natter and he concentrated on serving the thirsty punters.

Twice during the course of the evening he had occasion to go to the cellar building to change barrels but there was no sign of the barrels delivered that afternoon. He knew that such large items couldn't just disappear and was more suspicious than ever about the locked door in the cellar which Maria had said held spirits. He was convinced that was the only place they could be and decided he would have to place the pub under surveillance after closing time.

Before then, Paul Mitchell came in with yet more problems for Gary but due to the shortage of bar staff – it was Maria's night off and only he and Mr Stephano were serving – it wasn't until after the bell had rung that Gary could get an opportunity to talk to him.

"What's up then?" he asked the young lad who was staring aimlessly into a glass of lager. Gary cleared away empty glasses and ashtrays as Paul struggled to make himself heard amongst the pub's general hubbub.

"A friend of mine has been killed in a road accident."

"I'm sorry." Gary placed a reassuring hand on his shoulder. He was hopeless in cases such as this. "You were obviously close to one another."

"Went to the same school" the youngster said. "He worked at Justine's'"

"Ah – the nightclub owned by Mr Cowling?"

"Yeah that's right. Look I've something to tell you Mr Barker; it could be important."

Gary took a seat next to him.

"What is it?" he asked quietly.

"I promised my friend I wouldn't let on but now that he's dead ....." The lad left the sentence unfinished. Gary waited patiently.

"Its just that some bastard hit and run driver killed him and I think it may have been deliberate. Eddie, my mate, had a video and we used to watch certain videos round at his place."

"Certain videos?"

"Well – eh yes. They were pornographic." Paul looked across at Gary to see his reaction.

"I see. Nothing to be embarrassed about," Gary said with sincerity. He knew how inquisitive eighteen year old teenagers could be and could well remember his own introduction to the subject.

"He borrowed the videos from the nightclub and was always bragging to me about how Mr Cowling ran an operation upstairs at the club after 2am, when the club would normally close. Part of his job was giving out special 'tickets' for cash to those that asked for them during the evening and he also said something about the fact that they'd always be able to get away with it. You understand Mr Barker my concern for Eddie – I think the accident may well have been arranged!"

"Have you told anyone else this Paul?" asked Gary

"No. I wasn't sure what to do about it."

"Listen carefully. On no account mention this to anybody and I don't want you getting involved with that nightclub. This is a job for the police but it needs to be kept quiet. I know just the person to speak to and I promise it will be thoroughly investigated. Look I've got to go now - Mr Stephano's giving me strange looks! I'll keep in touch!"

Gary continued with his collecting of glasses and returning them to the bar. As he cleared the Inspector's table, he whispered in the officer's ear to wait for him outside the pub after closing.

****

It was getting colder. Not only could Gary tell by the numbness in his feet and hands but also by the steadily increasing specks of permafrost creeping across the windscreen of the GTI. He glanced again at the luminous dial of the car clock. 3am and still nothing had happened. Perhaps after all his theory was wrong and if something did not happen soon, he wouldn't be able to see anything through the frosted windows anyway.

He thought of Jacky tucked up warm in bed and the look in her eye when he'd told here he was going back to the pub on surveillance. She thought he was mad of course and had told him so before leaving him in the car and storming down the pathway towards the guesthouse. The sight of her long legs had almost led to him changing his mind and now, as he stared out into the blackness, he had to admit she was right. He didn't really have anything to go on but neither did Dougie Peters!

There little chat after the pub had closed revealed that Mr Stephano had admitted to a meeting with Mr Mitchell on the night of his death and that the accountant had left at midnight with the pub's books. According to the inspector, Sgt Grainger had taken a statement but felt there was nothing suspicious to report. Mr Mitchell had apparently been in good spirits when he'd left and the Stephano's were as surprised as anyone to hear of his murder.

Gary for his part had passed on the information from Paul concerning the suspicion of pornographic film shows being shown late at night at Justine's'. The Inspector had promised to look into it but frankly doubted that this was the case. He had a police officer regularly visiting the premises and would need substantiating evidence if he was to organise a raid. Gary wondered whether he should mention the 'incident' he'd had with Cowling and how PC Almond had just happened to be there.

He thought better of it as he wasn't sure Peters would take too kindly to his insinuation that maybe the police had a 'bent' copper in their midst!

A noise from the pub's car park, opposite, jolted him back to reality and something flashed across the road in front of him. 'Just a cat' he mused but then he heard it again. It was the sound of metal being scraped across the ground, first individually and then collectively. He strained his eyes through the driver's window and could see torch lights flashing around. Before he knew it, a black shadow swept by the car and continued until it stopped alongside the car park. It was then Gary realised it was a truck without lights that had coasted down the hill. The darkness and the frost on the windows hindered him and he wound down the driver's side screen. He couldn't however, make out any of the figures that were loading the heavy barrels onto the back of the lorry. The operation was over in two minutes and Gary watched as the truck slowly began to move further down the incline. The flashlights had disappeared as quickly as they had arrived. Gary presumed the holders had returned to the pub.

Without knowing why, the detective leapt out of the car and started chasing the lorry, his trainers making no sound on the tarmac road surface. The vehicle was gathering pace as it approached the bottom of the hill and as it did so the engine roared into life and the rear lights flowed.

With a combination of a leap and a dive, Gary's frozen fingers wrapped agonisingly over the rim of the lorry's tailgate. For a full second he felt himself being half dragged behind the vehicle before, with a superhuman effort he managed to find the strength from somewhere to lift himself up, over and into its rear where he fell into a crumpled heap.

At first he thought he'd made a complete fool of himself as the lorry appeared to be empty but as he gingerly felt his way along, he came across a tarpaulin. Moments later, he was underneath it and nearer the front he stumbled into a metal container, followed by a further five. Making himself comfortable as best he could in the cold surroundings – he squatted down amongst them and prepared to wait but for what he had no idea!

Chapter Thirteen

The journey had been short and Gary was grateful for that. His body was cold and his muscles ached from the continual pounding against the barrels, as the lorry thundered on its journey. He'd passed the time trying to see out from underneath the tarpaulin. The blackness however made it impossible to fathom out the vehicle's route but it appeared that their destination was to be set in the heart of the countryside, judging by the state of some of the roads they were travelling on.

After some thirty minutes, the narrow lanes and muddied tracks opened out onto a rough concrete plateau and the lorry sped across this before coming to a halt outside a large imposing building.

Gary heard a few words being exchanged between the driver and another unidentifiable voice before the lorry inched its way forward into the building. He waited, ears cocked and ready to pounce should the situation demand it but the engine died and nothing happened. Eventually, he heard the footsteps of the driver retreating in the distance and everything was still.

Cautiously he lifted a section of the tarpaulin and peered out. He appeared to be in old aircraft hangar, sparsely lit but full of various merchandise ranging from wooden chests to cardboard boxes piled high, one on top of the other.

The detective knew that this would probably be his only opportunity to escape the confines of the lorry before discovery. Carefully and with his heart in his mouth, he clambered over the side of the truck and slid effortlessly to the ground.

His trainers made no noise as he sprinted for the confines of heavy-duty racking and a secluded zone within the warehouse. It was only a trip of twenty yards but it was more than sufficient to raise his heart rate to that similar to a train rushing through a tube station. Crouching beside a pallet, containing cans of fizzy orange, he looked over at the deserted lorry and beyond to a lit office where he could see two men enjoying a smoke and a cup of coffee. The sight made him thirsty and he tore at the plastic covering the cans and extracted one. The tangy liquid refreshed him whilst he surveyed the corner of the hangar that he found himself in.

To his surprise he discovered he was amongst a great quantity of metal beer barrels all labelled 'Brennards Beers – Amsterdam' and stacked high in twos and threes. They were all similar to the type used at the Compton Arms. Gary circled around them. He tried to lift one or two but they appeared full and wouldn't budge.

Taking care to ensure that he was always hidden from view by keeping a container between him and the office, he continued to move around checking the barrels. He estimated there were over a hundred but he could find no means of checking what in fact they contained. In view of the secrecy and late-night manoeuvres at the Compton Arms, he was convinced it was something other than beer. Anyway, apart from that, what were so many barrels of a West Country Ale doing in an aircraft hangar in the middle of the Cotswolds?

It was while he was checking these barrels that the attack came. One moment his right arm was lifting a container, checking the weight and the next it was clamped tight between the jaws of a Doberman Pincher. It happened that fast!

The decision as to what to do to overcome the beast was taken from him by the dog's handler. The vice-like grip of the canine molars, were instantly replaced by the snapping of a set of handcuffs. He was frisked before being roughly prodded towards the office by a thick-set man in some sort of uniform.

The man continued to prod him from behind as they climbed up a wooden staircase where they were confronted by a half panelled, glass door. On the grime ridden olive-green paintwork, Gary noticed the words 'MIX-EX UK GOODS INWARDS' before he found himself unceremoniously shoved into the office.

For a moment the two occupants stood there staring at him, surprised by the abrupt manner of his entrance. It was the smaller of the two who Gary reckoned was the lorry driver, who spoke first.

"What have you got there, Bill?" he asked. The man had a crooked mouth which when he spoke, made it look as though he was sneering. Gary wondered for no apparent reason what sort of effect this would have on women. 'Probably have them screaming for the cops'.

"Found him snooping around the Brennards stuff," said his captor. "What should I do with him?"

"Dump him in the corner and handcuff him to the radiator pipe. I'll have to take advice!" To the other man he said

"You'd better go with Bill and check out whether he's brought any friends with him!"

The detective was forced over to the far corner of the office where he was instructed to sit on the floor. The cuffs were quickly transferred from the uniformed man's wrists to a pipe at ground level. Almost immediately Gary could feel the intense heat of the pipe against his exposed skin and he winced with pain.

In the meantime the lorry driver had dialled a number and Gary listened intently to the conversation whilst struggling to move his wrist away from the heat source.

"We've got a snooper here," the man said and looked across at him.

"Black man, 6ft or thereabouts – looks fit, grey hair – thirtyish"

The voice on the other end could be heard to be clearly raised and annoyed. The man looked inquisitively at Gary. His face had a redness of one who drank too much whisky.

"Your name Barker by any chance?" he questioned.

Gary nodded. He saw little point in dragging it out. The pipe was firmly embedded into a brick surround and the cuff was of solid steel. There was little chance of his immediate escape and he didn't fancy a 'kicking' just for this little weasel's gratification.

"Seems to be one and the same" the man said back into the mouthpiece before hanging up.

"well, well, well Mr Barker. You really have put my bosses back up with your interference. He's coming over to see you personally. Apparently you have already met, only this time I don't think the meeting will be so cordial."

"Would your bosses name be Patrick Wainwright by any chance?" asked Gary.

"Very clever of you Mr Barker"

"Not really. I thought I recognised his booming voice on the other end. Didn't sound too pleased did he?"

"I doubt that you'll have a lot to be pleased about when he gets here either. Wouldn't surprise me if a certain private detective doesn't end up as a concrete pillar on the M25!"

"Hasn't that already been built?" said Gary sarcastically and then regretted it as a well aimed boot struck him in the ribs.

"*I* make the jokes," said the man. "Just remember that you're not in a position to do otherwise."

The man returned to a desk cluttered with paperwork and sat down with his back towards Gary. He picked up the key, which the guard had left for the cuffs and placed it in the right hand drawer. From the other drawer he pulled out a girlie magazine and began thumbing through the pages. Every so often he'd look up and out of the office window at the merchandise below, before casting a cursory glance behind at the kidnapped victim. Having satisfied himself that the detective posed no threat, he returned to the magazine.

****

It was 10am by the time Wainwright arrived. Gary was by then in great pain from the burns on his wrist, which was now bleeding and in need of medical attention. He was also perspiring from the concentrated heat and for the umpteenth time wiped his brown and chin with the back of his freed left arm. The time had dragged like one serving a life sentence and it was quite a relief to see the 'elephant man' crash his way through the flimsy excuse of an office door.

"Where is he?" Wainwright gruffed and then seeing Gary rendered immobile in the corner, confidently approached him.

"We meet again Mr Barker. Interfering is something you might not live to regret. How did you find out about his place?" The voice was controlled but demanding.

Wainwright towered over him. The man for once was wearing a shirt and tie but the shirt was ill-fitted – so much so that his paunched belly protruded through the gap between the lower two buttons which were straining the limits of the eyelets.

From his dominated position, the detective looked up at the bulldog-like face. He hadn't noticed before in the offices of Enterprise Transport but the man had pock marks on the right cheek, similar to a severe case of acne.

"Don't make it difficult on yourself Barker" Wainwright remonstrated. "I say again – how did you get here?"

"Followed the smell," said Gary. "Stretches all the way from the Compton Arms."

Wainwright's expression changed to one of alarm. From his point of view it was obvious the detective knew too much. He turned to the smaller man who had been guarding Barker.

"Where's Bill and Foggy?" he demanded.

"Well – they're off shift now boss. They've gone home"

"Shit. The stuff's been delivered hasn't it Mack?"

"Yes boss. Its on the lorry below."

"You mean its not been unloaded?"

"Well no. When we found this 'dick' here, Foggy and Bill went off to check that he'd not brought any others with him. They then went off shift and I couldn't unload it on my own; it'd break my back to try" the man pleaded in defence.

"Get down there now. I'll be down in a minute." As the

lorry driver left, Wainwright snatched at the phone and dialled.

"Problems" he said into the mouthpiece "we've got big problems. Yes we've the shipment here all right, there's only one more outstanding and that's in hand but we're going to have to bring the timetable forward – that bloody private detective I've talked to you about has poked his nose in and I've got him tied up here at the warehouse. What the hell do you suggest I do with him?"

Gary strained hard to hear the muffled voice coming through in reply. It was unmistakably female and he had a sneaking suspicion who it was.

"Right" said Wainwright, having received his instructions. "I'll put it into effect." Replacing the receiver, he shuffled round to his victim. Gary thought he looked a tired man. The face was that of one overcome by too much stress, the forehead was heavily furrowed and the eyes heavy and sunken.

"You'll be relieved to hear Mr Barker that you have a slight reprieve but don't get your hopes up too much – I emphasise the slight."

"Pack it in now Wainwright. Give yourself up. There's still a chance you could get off with a light sentence man. Don't be a fool. I know that whatever you're shipping has got to be illegal and that is tied up with the murder of Herbert Mitchell and how do you know that I've not already contacted the police?"

The big man considered what the detective was saying. Gary could almost see his brain ticking over.

"No you couldn't have done that. They'd have been here before now and anyhow they'd need evidence and you haven't got a thing. No, nice try Barker but by the time the police do work it out, we'll be long gone."

Wainwright covered the short distance to the radiator and began turning down the control.

"I'm afraid Mack's a sadistic buggar," he said. "I may be a cruel sod too but by the state of your wrist I think he's already punished you enough.

With that final remark he left the office, presumably to assist Mack with the unloading of the six Brennards barrels.

Gary closed his eyes and drifted into a state of semi-consciousness trying to work out things in his mind. Why was Mitchell murdered? What was the connection with the books? Was the accountant involved and killed because he threatened to expose Wainwright and his friends? Who are MID-EX UK? Is Cowling up to his neck in it to? And how did Candy Roberts fit into all this, because he was convinced that was who Wainwright had been talking to on the phone!

****

"Wake up Gary for goodness sake!" The voice commanded urgently and he could feel himself being shaken violently. He raised his head and eyes to see Jacky knelt on the floor before him.

The relief on her face was evident and surprised as he was to see the beautiful girl, he knew time was short and Wainwright could be back at any moment.

"Top right drawer." The words gushed out of him. "A key quick!"

She was a smart kid he thought, cool under pressure. Within seconds he was freed from the pipe. There wasn't time at this juncture to enquire how she'd found him – the main object was to escape but how?

"Listen," he said "they'll be back any minute. Hide under the desk by the window and take the coffee pot with you. I'll lie here by the pipe to make it look as though I'm still handcuffed. Wait until I say 'now', and hit the man nearest you as hard as you can over the head. I'll tackle the other one. Got it?"

"Yes," she said "are you all right – you're bleeding badly"

"Its nothing – just do as you're told"

Gary watched as she took up her position underneath the

desk. For once she was wearing a sensible pair of jeans coupled with a chunky sweater. He knew he shouldn't be thinking it but he was trying to imagine what she would look like crouched under the desk in a mini skirt and black stockings riding high on her thighs. A delectable thought of course but highly impracticable given the circumstances.

They did not have long to wait. It was Wainwright that first staggered through the door, his shirt clinging to his chest, the result of perspiration from lifting the heavy barrels off the lorry. His assistant Mack, the smaller of the two, followed from behind like a faithful puppy.

"When Bill gets back you'd better shift the lorry back to the depot," said Wainwright. "In the meantime its time I made tracks." He walked over towards Gary talking as he went. "And you'd better make sure that he's closely watched at all times."

The man stood bent over Gary with his hands on his knees.

"Don't think we'll be meeting again Mr Barker," he said gloatingly.

"I wouldn't count on it," said Gary. "Now" he shouted. As he screamed out the word, his right leg kicked viciously upward into the man's groin. A look of half pain and half bewilderment came over Wainwright's face. It lasted a fraction of a second before his hands moved from his knees to where the pain from the kick and landed. The detective was quickly on his feet and followed up the kick with a sweeping movement from the back of his clenched fist. There was a sound of knuckle on jaw and the big man's head rocked back.

His partner Mack stooped to the floor, his hand scrabbling at a loose floorboard. As Wainwright collapsed onto his back from the velocity of Gary's backhand punch, the detective faced up to the other man's confrontation. The arm holding a gun was rising rapidly from the gaping hole in the floor. It never reached waist level as his face took the full blow from the coffee pot that Jacky was holding. The full anger of the woman was expressed by the way the man's nose was flattened to his face revealing exposed bone and lashes of blood.

"You bitch," said the man spitting flecks of blood through his lips as the blood streamed down his face. She stood there shocked by the results of her assault and it was Gary who intervened by grabbing the arm holding the gun and forcing it upward. There was a 'crack' into the ceiling as the gun fired and the two men struggled back towards the doorway.

Gary appeared to have the upper hand in terms of height and strength as he laid into the smaller man with blow after blow to his chest. Mack was not without courage and though being forced back by the punches, he wouldn't concede the fight.

The detective was winning the battle, when he lost his balance. His foot disappeared into the hole left exposed after the removal of the gun and Mack took the advantage by pacing backwards out through the door. He raised the gun and pointed it at Gary's belly. His crouching style and bloodied face made him look like some creature from a horror movie.

Gary took evasive action by throwing his body to one side. The respite was temporary as a bullet whistled past his ear, shattering a pane of glass in the office window behind him.

There was a short death-like scream from the gunman and when Gary looked through the door again, the man had disappeared. He hauled his leg out from the floorboard and rushed to the short platform at the top of the stairs outside the office. Looking down from the single rail at the warehouse floor below, he saw the man slumped on his side beside which a pool of blood was quickly forming. By backing out in the crouched position, the man had taken one pace too many and in a state of nervous tension had forgotten his position. One second there had been firm foundations under his feet and the next – thin air!

After handcuffing Wainwright, who was still unconscious, to the same pipe as he himself had endured, Gary and Jacky dismounted the office staircase. The girl stood to one side as the detective checked the body for signs of life. As he did so, they both heard the sound of an approaching vehicle.

Gary's eyes scanned the warehouse. Seeing a tarpaulin close

by he grabbed it and hastily covered the body, before seizing Jacky by the hand. Together they made a dash for a place of safety.

They watched as a man in chauffeur's uniform entered through the doorway with a tall, pencil-slim man dressed in a smart double-breasted cream suit. He was wearing a panama hat, had a long thin cigarette holder in his mouth from which a cloud of smoke lingered in the still air of the warehouse.

The thin man stopped just inside the warehouse door as if sensing something. He motioned to the chauffeur and the man produced a cloth, which he used to wipe mud off his white shoes, before handing it back to the other man. The two of them then proceeded towards the staircase and Gary and Jacky took the opportunity to sneak out.

The Golf GTI sped niftily along the country lanes heading towards Etherton. Though she was driving fast Gary felt perfectly safe in the passenger seat. The excitement of the last few minutes had given Jacky a controlled air that up until now he had never fully appreciated. She was talking and driving with admirable confidence.

"When I discovered this morning," she said "that you had not returned from your all night vigil at the Compton Arms, I returned there and found the car abandoned. I wasn't sure what to do, but then I remembered your concern about the beer barrels travelling between Enterprise Transport and the pub, so I drove down to the transport depot and waited. I felt a bit of a fool because I had no idea what I was doing there and I was very worried about you. I did not intend to stay long and was debating whether to call the police or have a word with the boss of Enterprise Transport, when a car shot out of the depots yard. So I followed it all the way to the warehouse on an old deserted airfield. I parked the car well away and carefully approached. There was a lorry in the warehouse with beer barrels on it and I could also see many others stacked on the floor. Looking up at the office I saw two men. I felt sure that you were in there too, because they kept looking down at the floor of the office as if a third person was in there with them. I had to wait of course until they came down to unload the lorry, before nipping up the stairs. Looking through the window I could see you shackled to the pipe and that's when I made my move."

"And" stressed Gary "not a moment too soon." He was listening intently to what she was saying but at the same time was considering what should be his next move. Contacting Inspector Peters seemed the most logical, especially given the untimely death of the lorry driver. This would however take matters completely out of his hands and might actually jeopardise the whole operation. It seemed pointless to involve the police. What would they do? The warehouse would be raided by them and what would they find – sweet F.A." Wainwright and the 'white-suited' man would certainly have disappeared, as would the body. They might of course find some illicit contraband but not the organisation behind it and besides, there was a further shipment to come. The more he considered it, the less he felt inclined to impart the information – not at this stage!

"I said – what do you think they're shifting, have you gone deaf?" asked Jacky.

"What? Sorry love I was thinking. Difficult to say, could be anything from guns to drugs. Look let's get back to Mrs Haines. I need a bath and change of clothes"

"What about the police?"

"In time," said Gary. "All in good time."

Chapter Fourteen

There were two messages awaiting Gary back at Mrs Haines. One was from Inspector Peters asking him to telephone and the other was a typewritten note with no signature. It merely stated 'NEXT TIME – LUCKY'.

It was the note that worried him. He knew he would have to be on his guard. It must refer to the shot fired at him. Gary was being warned that next time would be for real!"

Soaking in the bath had however, done him a world of good. The stiffness in the joints had been eased and the stinging sensation in his damaged wrist relieved. It had also stimulated his brain cells. He always found he could think a lot clearer after the pores of his skin had been opened up by rising steam. The time in the bath had been put to good use though, as the jotted notes revealed. With all that had happened to him since arriving in Etherton, he was now convinced that the answers he needed must be related to the Compton Arms.

As he dressed in front of the wall mirror, his eyes kept glancing to the list, which he'd slipped in behind it.

a. Mitchell – accountant – murdered – books.
b. His last client Stephano – Compton Arms.
c. Shipment barrels from Compton Arms to warehouse – Brennards barrels.
d. Locked room Compton Arms – what behind it?
e. Is Cowling involved? – Pornographic film shows after hours!
f. Patrick Wainwright, Candy Roberts – seen at Compton Arms – how do they fit in?
g. Man in white suit – who is he? What connection?
h. Final shipment still to be delivered – from where?

****

"My aren't we handsome!" said Jacky, standing in the bathroom doorway admiring him. Gary pulled on a crisp white shirt over his naked chest and nonchalantly buttoned it up. He could feel her eyes staring at him.

"I just love the contrast between your black body and a white shirt; it brings out the animal in you," she giggled. Jacky continued to watch as he tucked the shirttails into a pair of tailored jeans. When he was finished he took her into his arms and they stood and hugged one another for a few moments before he spoke.

"Listen my little heroine, I've a job for you. I want you to contact Paul Mitchell. You'll probably find him at home, the telephone number is Etherton 41027 or alternatively he'll be at Compton Post Office. When you find him I want the two of you to trace Candy Roberts and tail her. Begin with Mitchell and Roberts the accountants. If she's not there try her boutique shop and as a last resort Enterprise Transport. Now, Paul is an eager amateur but we're up against some nasty characters, so no visits and let me know if she makes contact with Patrick Wainwright. Good girl!" He kissed her on the cheek, reached for his jacket and started to leave.

"Where will you be so I can contact you?" she called as he darted down the stairs.

"Compton Arms or here"

"Take care," she shouted

"And you," came the feint reply.

****

The pub was surrounded by police cars. It was only 2pm and

the customers were all outside in the car park, huddled in little groups debating what was going on.

Gary recognised PC Almond as one of the officers' on the door, who was ensuring no one would re-enter. Remembering their altercation in Cowling's office at the nightclub, he strolled boldly up to him and said

"Inspector Peters wants to see me. He is here?"

The officer eyed him suspiciously. There was a slight pause before he responded.

"You'd better go in sir," and politely he held open the door for him. "You'll have to walk all the way through the pub to the rear and cross over to the separate building. You'll find him in the cellar."

The detective thanked him and followed his instructions. He was 'greeted', if that is the right word, by a tearful Maria who was being consoled by a woman police officer on a bench seat in the public bar.

Gary approached her but was unceremoniously waved aside by the policewoman.

"I don't know who you are," she said curtly "but Mrs Stephano is, as you can see, in no position to talk."

The detective paused. He instinctively knew that something serious had happened to Maria Stephano's husband. Her distressed state and the abundance of police activity led him to believe it was pointless to continue his charade impersonating a barman.

"I'm a private investigator," he said. "You can check with Inspector Peters if you like."

The policewoman was used to dealing with the likes of him in her role of comforting distressed victims.

"I don't care if you're the Pope," she said. "This is neither the time or place. Detective Inspector Peters is out through the back of the pub." She indicated his dismissal by a definite pointing of her arm towards the rear door.

"No – wait." The voice was choked with emotion but the tear-stained face of Maria lifted itself from behind the concealed hands. As she did so, light reflected off the largest stone amongst the array of rings and it briefly sparkled.

"You really a detective?" she asked.

"Yes. I'm sorry for deceiving you. I've been hired by Mrs Mitchell. You'll know what its about ....." He allowed the statement to fade, offering her the opportunity of responding.

A half-smile crossed her lips.

"I thought you might be something of the sort," she said. "You make a lousy barman!"

She used a handkerchief to wipe her reddened eyes but only succeeded in smearing the mascara into a streak across her high cheekbone.

Gary pulled up a stool from the bar and sat closely facing the two ladies. He acknowledged the look of caution from the police officer.

"Maria," he said, in a controlled and easy manner. "Can you tell me what's happened here?"

The words came gushing out in a torrent of store-up emotion.

"Edwardo - he's dead. Out there, in the cellar! I told him not to get involved."

"Involved? Involved with whom?" Gary demanded.

"I – I can't say. He may come back. It could be me next!"

"Maria listen. I know this place is being used for storing some sort of contraband. Edwardo was in on it too wasn't he?"

She nodded.

"Was Mitchell involved as well?"

"No," she said emphatically. "He had nothing to do with this. He was a nice kind man – you must believe that!" Her eyes pleaded with him and Gary nodded.

"Yes – yes of course," he said. "I'm sure he was. Tell me," he asked quietly. "What was being stored here?"

"I don't know, I honestly don't know. Edwardo had the keys and he never told me. All he said was, we were being well paid for it and to tell no one."

"All right Maria. Don't distress yourself."

The policewoman looked up at Gary and added. "I think you've had more than you're entitled to."

"Thank you," said Gary politely. "Thank you both."

From the looks of Stephan's body, someone had certainly beaten the daylights out of him. The face was barely recognisable, a twisted contortion of blood and bone resembling a cheese, ham and tomato pizza. Such a sight would have turned many a strong man's stomach and even a man conditioned to seeing victims of violence such as Gary, was relieved when the Inspector replaced the cover over the head.

"Poor sod," said Peters. "Strange thing is that despite the battering it looks likely that his actual death was an accident."

"How do you mean?" asked Gary, taking in the near empty space of the cellar's storeroom. It would have been empty, bar one Brennards beer-barrel and of course Stephano's body.

"I'm only surmising Barker," Peters continued but as you can see the man had taken a considerable hammering, presumably after being forced to open the store-room door. And yet you will observe blood on the side of that barrel, leading to the pool around his head. It looks as though as he fell from the blows thumping into him, that the back of his head struck the rim of the metal barrel. The haemorrhaging I reckon proved fatal. We'll know more of course after the post mortem."

"What's in the barrel?" asked Gary, stepping over the body and easing his way toward it. The room was cramped with the three of them. He was thinking that such a room would barely hold more than six barrels such as he'd seen loaded onto the lorry the previous night.

"Nothing – its empty," said Peters blandly.

"Mind if I look?"

"Help yourself. It's been dusted for prints. In fact we're about through here for now. Was about to leave when you arrived. Have you anything further for me on the Mitchell case?"

"Maybe"

Gary lifted the barrel easily. As the Inspector had said, it felt empty but in view of what had been happening at both the pub and the warehouse, he wasn't prepared to leave it there!

He replaced it on the floor and clambered onto it in order to see the top shelf which was set at fingertip reach when seen standing from the floor. It too appeared empty, until he ran his hands along the wooden surface. His fingers touched something cold and using his nails, he scrabbled into the wood to reveal a flat metal object some two feet long. He extracted it and climbed down.

The object was a giant tool, similar to a spanner.

"Look at this," he said triumphantly. "Hand made – look at the welding. I reckon it probably fits onto the spigots of a barrel like this."

He inserted the tool into the centre of the barrel where it clicked firmly into place and turned it anti-clockwise until he could turn it no longer. Gripping hold of the tool he then lifted and surprisingly the top of the barrel came away in one piece.

The two men peered in. Halfway down was a metal ring. The barrel had been split into two compartments and Gary tugged on the ring, which held the lower half. There was some resistance as it covered a rubbery suction seal but with extra effort the metal casing came away in his hands and he pulled the lid out. As expected the barrel looked empty but a small object caught his eye and reaching right down into the bottom, he retrieved it.

"A bullet!" exclaimed Inspector Peters.

"Yes and that's not all Inspector – it's a 'live' round. No doubt at some stage this barrel contained far more than beer. Its been separated in order to transport contraband in the bottom and beer in the top."

"Smuggling"

"Of a sort and I've a good idea of some of the protagonists!"

"Protagonists," exclaimed the Inspector. "Where the heck did you pick up a word like that?"

"Shakespeare of course – leading players that sort of thing."

"I know what the word means. I'm not a complete idiot.

Just wondered where someone like you would have picked it up."

Gary ignored the Inspector's friendly jibe. The pieces of the jigsaw in the case were gradually coming together and his mind was actively engaged in working out the next moves.

"Did you get any further with the information I gave you concerning pornographic film shows at Justine's'?" he asked.

"Now now Barker. For god's sake you can see I've a murder enquiry to get under way. What with this and the Mitchell thing don't you think I've not got more important things to worry about than a blue movie show!"

"But they could be connected," Gary interjected. "What about this false barrel here. It's obvious surely that it's been used for transporting small arms. Isn't it also possible that other undesirable materials could be carried in the same way. Things like drugs or even 'porno' movies for example."

"Well eh yes. I suppose it is. Hadn't quite thought of it like that. You think this pub might be a 'pick-up' point is that it?"

Gary waited for the penny to drop in the Inspector's mind. He himself was thinking about all the Brennards beer barrels he'd seen at the warehouse. If they all contained half beer and half goods, then a big shipment was imminent for onward transportation and in view of his lucky escape it was clearly also evident that those barrels would now be shifted promptly. Time was getting short. It was time he acted! He remembered what Maria had said about Edwardo being well paid for storing things. 'Proof' he thought to himself. 'Proof' of a connection that's it!

"Inspector follow me," he ordered.

With the information supplied by Maria, they forced open the drawer of the desk belonging to Mr Stephano in his cramped office set at the top of the stairs above the public lounge.

As he rifled through the various papers with his 'good' hand, Gary filled the Inspector in with the events of the previous evening. Peters for his part relayed the information through direct by telephone to the West Midlands Regional Crime Squad.

"MID-EX UK is the name of the company," he transmitted. "You'll have to check it out and arrange for an operations code Al Priority. Yes I know you'll need authority so check later with the Chief Constable but we'll need raids organised on all the company's listed branches. Put out a 'stop and search' on any lorry having a Mid-Ex UK connection or carrying Brennards Beers as well." He replaced the receiver, only to have to pick it up again.

"Its for you," he said gruffly, handing it to Gary. "Look, I'll use the intercom in the car. You've stirred up a hornet's nest and no mistake. I've a lot of calls to make and some explaining to do. I just hope your right Barker, otherwise I could find myself back pounding a beat which at my age could prove fatal."

Gary grabbed the phone from the elder man whilst continuing to flick through the piles of 'junk' correspondence, which he'd removed from the drawers and placed on the desk.

"Who is it?" he said sharply into the mouthpiece. "What – Where? Eureka," he said pouncing on a particular piece of paper and then into the mouthpiece added, "Give me the registration mark."

He jotted down the details before adding "Stay where you are Jacky – I'll be five minutes."

****

The Inspector listened intently as the Rover powered swiftly through Compton village heading for Etherton.

"Very recent paying-in slip for £1000 into Stephano's bank account," said Gary excitedly "the reverse of which shows it was a single cheque payment from Patrick Wainwright. It would be interesting to know what that payment was for, now wouldn't it?"

"That's as may be but it doesn't constitute proof. Could have bought a car for example," said Peters.

"Ah," continued Gary "but Stephano kept good accounts. I found this little notelet book amongst the papers appertaining to 'commissions' received ME." ME could stand for Mid-Ex. I reckon a good accountant could establish a connection if we can get our hands on Wainwright's records. Don't forget I am a witness to his movements at the aircraft hangar yesterday." Gary nurtured his injured hand ruefully. "Finally," he said, "I wormed a confession out of his skinny little secretary. She came into the pub the other evening; I brought her a few drinks and she let-on that the business of Enterprise Transport appeared precarious financially to say the least. However, a little liquid persuasion and she did let loose the fact that she'd seen another bank account which was apparently very flush with funds."

"Really," said Peters "now that is interesting." He reached for the radio control receiver, his eyes never leaving the road ahead.

"Control. Inspector Peters on route to Etherton bank for surveillance on subjects Patrick Wainwright and Candy Roberts, last seen driving red Jaguar 'S' saloon, registration mark E428 OWL."

"Copy Inspector," came the response. "Sgt Grainger here sir. Chief Constable has been put in the picture, asks whether you need more manpower."

"Negative, Sergeant at this juncture, but ask for back-up to be put on standby. In the meantime I want you to personally check-up on Jeremiah Cowling at Justine's nightclub. Go in under the guise of checking-up on PC Almond's crime prevention work. Afterwards keep a man posted on his movements. Understood?"

"What am I supposed to be looking for sir?"

"This is between you and me Sergeant. Is there anyone else with you?" There was some background activity as people left the control room.

"Not now sir," came the reply.

"Good. I don't want things jeopardised and though we have our differences I do believe you're to be trusted."

"Thank you sir."

"It's possible that Cowling is using the nightclub for pornographic film shows and illegal gambling. Further evidence may come to light shortly. I'm sure you'll know to approach this case!"

"Yes sir – understood." There was a pause before the intercom again stuttered into life. "I thank you for your trust in me Inspector." The words were said with sincerity and the Inspector smiled to himself. Maybe Sgt Grainger and he could yet get along together. Stranger things had happened.

"A little friction there Inspector," said Gary hearing the tone of the conversation.

"Local humour," gruffed Peters. "Listen there is something you should know. We've discovered that the place where Mitchell was found 'Peaceful Waters' belongs to a Shane Phillips. It's been empty for the past six months. Mr Phillips works for British Aerospace in Saudi Arabia and consequently is home only once or twice a year."

"Shane Phillips?" queried Gary. "Any relevance?"

"Yes," said the Inspector dryly. "Candy Roberts' maiden name was Phillips. He's her brother!"

Chapter Fifteen

"Are they still in there?" questioned Gary. They'd parked the Rover outside Etherton Town Hall, which afforded them a distant view of the bank.

Jacky had seen them arrive and raced across the road to meet the two men. Further up the street, the Golf could be seen, with the shadowy outline of Paul Mitchell in the passenger seat. Even from this distance he looked skinny. Elsewhere the streets appeared to have an air of normality as shoppers went about their business.

"Yes," said Jacky somewhat puffed. Running in high heels was an awkward business. "They've been in some time – since I telephoned in fact."

"Counting and collecting a large sum of money is time consuming Miss," interjected Peters.

"You called me Jacky the other evening *Dougie*," she stressed, showing friendly admonishment.

"I wasn't on duty then miss"

"No – of course not – how silly of me! Far be it for me to presume that we were friends."

"Now don't start Jacky," said Gary. "Remember the poor Inspector's ulcer. We don't want to play it up now do we?"

As if touching a raw nerve Peters reached into his pocket and pulled out a packet of mints.

"Job like this is enough to give anyone ulcers," he muttered.

"Right, tell me how you tracked them down," said Gary, his dark features barely two inches from the contrasting white flesh tones of her terribly English face as she poked her head through the passenger side window of the car.

"Look it's cold out here Gary. Can't I get in the back?"

"No you can't love. From here on the professionals take

over and it could get a little nasty. I don't want to take the risk of having you with us should we have to make a quick getaway!"

"Spoilsport," she said. "Paul and I do the leg-work and you chaps take the glory."

"That's the way it is Miss," said Peters sucking on the mint.

"Well there was nothing to it really," Jacky said. She turned up the collar of her suede coat to avoid the wind chill. Already one side of her face was reddening. "Found them both at Candy's boutique; followed them for a brief visit to Enterprise Transport and then onto the bank. Then I called for you."

"Good girl." He looked across at Peters before continuing. "With the Inspector's permission, here's the plan as I see it. I think if we follow Roberts and Wainwright they may well lead us to whoever is responsible for their little operation. Jacky – I want you to take Paul with you to the Compton Arms. In view of the death of Mr Stephano, the landlady is going to be short staffed and there is still a pub to be run. Try and sort something out! I'm sure she'll understand when she realises the predicament Mrs Stephano is in. Have you got that?"

"Yes oh master," said Jacky sarcastically. "Anything your lordship commands!"

Gary pulled her head roughly towards him and kissed her firmly on the lips. She smelt of fresh honeysuckle and he was reluctant to draw away.

"Uh – hem," interrupted Peters "activity at the bank"

Gary gave her another peck on the lips before winding the window up, leaving the girl with a look of astonishment.

"Take care," he heard her muffled voice say, before Peters gently eased the Rover away from the Town Hall kerbside and out into the mainstream of traffic.

The detective gave her a final wave before checking his watch. It was now 3.05pm. It would start getting dark soon and he hoped Roberts and Wainwright did not have far to travel. If it did come to a shoot-out he'd rather be in a position to see his targets. The thought was not lost on him and as the car gathered speed, he pulled out the Baretta and checked it was loaded.

Seeing it the Inspector uttered.

"Good god man – you don't think it will come to that do you?"

"I hope not, it's purely a precaution," he stated blandly.

"Have you got a licence for it?" asked Peters. It was an automatic response for a policeman to make given the circumstances.

"Bit late for that now, don't you think?"

The two men fell silent, each with their own thoughts. Three cars ahead of them, the red Jaguar began to pick up speed.

Chapter Sixteen

"I'm liking this less and less," gruffed Peters. "It's beginning to look like a wild goose chase. Maybe they've cottoned on to the fact we're following them?"

Gary said nothing. He too was getting concerned. The last hour of tailing the Jaguar had strained them both. It wasn't easy following a car for that length of time without being discovered – especially at speeds approaching 100mph.

The initial surveillance from Etherton to the M5 motorway had been easy enough, the slower traffic helping in keeping the quarry in sight at a two or three car distance. Motorway driving on the M5 and M6 however had been another matter and once or twice the Inspector had suggested they call in a motorway patrol car to ease the pressure.

Gary hadn't wanted that. He felt that Wainwright and the woman might be nervously forced into changing their plan of action – whatever it was. When they had merged onto the M6 at Birmingham, he too began having doubts. For some reason he assumed that whoever they were on their way to meet, would be closer by.

He'd felt a little better when the Jaguar left the motorway at Stoke-on-Trent but for the last twenty minutes the doubts had returned.

What were they doing driving across country on 'B' roads and apparently doubling back on themselves? Had they discovered they were being followed and if so what were they going to do about it?

The light now was fading fast. Gary checked his watch. It was 4pm – barely 20 minutes to sunset. Already the occasional passing car was displaying headlights and still there was no sign of the car ahead stopping.

He strained his eyes at the map through the diminishing light available. The road such as it was appeared to lead to nowhere but circled a piece of land tightly contoured. He gazed out of the window at the passing hedgerows and realised the car was now climbing gradually round a steep winding incline. There was little apparent in the way of civilisation. Ahead of them in the distance, he could make out the tail lights of the Jaguar glowing eerily.

"What do you reckon?" gruffed Peters again.

"Shit – I don't know," he retorted. "Maybe they've stashed some loot away around here and are going to collect!"

It was now Peters turn to say nothing. Since they'd left Etherton he'd been a worried man. This was way outside his jurisdiction and he knew he should have left it in the hands of the West Midlands Regional Crime Squad. Perhaps he'd made a mistake in following Barker's suggestion but he didn't really regret it. Middle age was fast approaching and opportunities for excitement since he'd been transferred from the city had been practically zero. He liked the detective and envied him his freedom to pick and choose the cases he worked on. Though the last hour of 'tailing' had been monotonous, he was surprised at how the adrenalin was still pumping him up. He'd missed that since his arrival in Worcestershire. How he was going to explain this 'incredible journey' to the Chief Constable was however another matter.

With these thoughts the car was driving itself on automatic pilot. Physically Peters was in control but mentally he was in another dimension. It was only when Gary tugged urgently at his arm that he realised the taillights in front had disappeared.

"Quick hard left!" he heard the detective say.

He swung the wheel to order. The tyres screeched as they scrabbled over some gravel and they were transported into another world.

All around them, as far as the eye could see, was what appeared to be a mass of grey concrete. Closer scrutiny by both men revealed row upon row of white lined spaces. They'd stumbled across the largest car park that either of them had ever seen.

"Where the hell are we?" muttered Peters.

"Looks like the world's largest Sainsburys," said Gary dryly. Spotting the taillights ahead he added. "Keep your distance Dougie!"

The Inspector eased his foot off the accelerator and the Rover crawled past the proliferation of empty car spaces. Slowly but surely they inched their way forward to some coloured lights twinkling through the twilight gloom. Further ahead Gary could make out more moving lights, which were trundling across the skyline at tree top level. As they got closer, he realised that these lights were the interiors of train compartments. He recalled he'd seen similar operations in the States when he'd lived there but this was his first experience of such a sight in Britain.

The nearer they approached, the more obvious it became that they had hit upon England's answer to Disneyland and the moving lights belonged to a monorail train.

"Of course," said the Inspector triumphantly. "Connington Towers." Only opened this summer. Didn't think it would be operating this time of year though!"

"That's why it's almost empty," said Gary, "too damn cold and according to a sign we've just passed, it closes for winter this weekend and more importantly at 5pm today!"

"That means if they are meeting someone here – they'll have to be quick about it."

Gary was about to say something when the taillights ahead flowed bright red.

"Look – they're parking," he said. "Pull in here for Christ's sake!"

"I'd better call for reinforcements," said Peters and he reached for the R.T.

"No – there isn't time. Quickly man – they're heading for the train!"

The two men alighted rapidly from the car. Immediately

they settled into an easy jog to reduce the distance between trackers and hunted.

The couple ahead were barely fifty yards distant now as they took the steps two at a time up towards the platform of the monorail terminus. As they did so, a train slowly approached on the opposite line and rounded the 'U' bend of the raised rail before guiding itself towards the small station's platform.

Wainwright and the girl appeared unhurried. As they followed behind in the thickening gloom of a November sky, Gary cast his eyes forwards towards the approaching mono-train. The machinery itself resembled a gigantic silver bullet as it appeared head-on from out of the bend and coasted silently through the station until all it's carriages were safely positioned alongside the raised platform. There was a 'whooshing' noise and the individual carriage doors slid open. No one alighted. The train to all intents and purposes appeared empty. It waited like a ghost train for it's next trip into the unknown.

As the pursued couple reached the top of the terminus staircase, the station's overhead lights captured them and it was only then that Gary could get a really good look.

She was dressed all in black. The legs which had previously excited him, were concealed in tight leather trousers and trainers. The top too was in the same material and with her back towards him, she looked like a slim version of a man. Only the yellow cascading hair betrayed her sex.

For his part, Wainwright's great bulk was for the most part concealed behind a brown suede coat, trimmed at the edges with white fur. In his left hand he carried a small red battered suitcase, similar to the one the Chancellor of the Exchequer presents on Budget Day. His other hand was otherwise occupied on the woman's shapely posterior as he guided her towards a compartment near the front of the train. She appeared not to notice this or chose to ignore it. Either way the gesture was not reciprocated and they stepped into the carriage and sat next to one another with their backs towards the station platform. Neither of them turned round.

The sliding doors began to close. It was obvious to Gary they could not make it in time to the same compartment and he sprinted for the next one where he jammed his foot in the doorway. Peters was right behind him.

The compartment was compact with individual bucket seat accommodation for twelve people and it was conservatively painted throughout in blue and white. It appeared deceivingly spacious due to the expanse of glass used in the carriage framework. There was a tight aisle between the seats and both Peters and Barker quickly forced their way through it and the empty carriage towards the connecting glass door.

They stood either side of it and looked in. As they did so the carriage began to move and the intercom played its pre-recorded message.

"Good afternoon. Welcome to Connington Towers. You are travelling on a monorail system, which will take you directly to Connington Station and the official entrance to the Theme Park. Journey time is approximately six minutes and we ask you to remain seated throughout and not to smoke. On arrival, please do not leave your seats until the train is stationary and the doors open. The park closes at 5pm and the staff at Connington Towers hope you will enjoy your stay."

"Bingo," said Gary thrusting his head back away from the glass door.

"What did you see?" asked the Inspector as the motion of the train threw him back against one of the seats. "God I hope this thing's safe," he added, turning to look through the window. "Did I tell you I'm not one for heights."

"It's him," said Gary, his hand reaching inside his jacket pocket to check on the Baretta. "The man who was at the warehouse – the Latin looking fellow in the white suit I told you about."

"Right," said Peters "so what's our next move?"

"What do you think?" Gary asked the question and indicated by means of his head and eyes towards the connecting door that he thought the move was obvious.

"You mean we break through and arrest all three?"

"Why not?"

"Surely it would be better to arrest them at the next station."

"What – and risk the chance of their escape. Look Dougie, we've got them banged to rights in a train compartment. How can they get away at this moment? Leave it until the station and we stand a great risk of them disappearing into the night. No it's now or never!"

The Inspector thought for a moment. He could see the sense in Gary's argument. Should they escape justice now, not only would he be resigned to Etherton for the rest of his career but there was a good chance the deaths of Herbert Mitchell and Edwardo Stephano would remain unsolved. As Barker had indicated to him in the Rover on the way here, the answers most definitely lay with Wainwright, Roberts and whoever it was they were meeting.

"Very well," he said meekly. "I don't like it but I agree, in the absence of reinforcements we appear to have little choice."

He ran his fingers through a troublesome lock of silvery hair that had dropped over his eyes. When he pulled his hand back, he wasn't that surprised to notice that the tips of his fingers were damp with a watery substance. He ran the back of his hand across the forehead to remove the beads of sweat.

Peters looked across at Barker. Damn the man! He looked so cool standing there, one hand in pocket, the other leaning nonchalantly against the side of the train's compartment. It was as if they were having a casual conversation about what they'd seen on TV the previous night. Until he pulled out the Baretta that was!

"I'll take Wainwright," Gary said. "I've a score to settle with him. You take our Latin friend – he's on your left as we're standing here now."

"What about the girl?"

Gary shrugged his shoulders.

"Guess we'll have to play that by ear," he said smilingly. The expression had the effect of highlighting his even white teeth against his dark skin. Peters did not know why, but he was stuck with a vision of a TV toothpaste commercial. He wondered why it was they never showed a black actor advertising toothpaste. Surely the contrast would be more effective.

The two men squared up to one another.

"Lets do it," said Gary.

****

The three occupants in the next carriage were actively engrossed in heated conversation as the combined efforts of Peters and Barker's shoulders forced the lock on the interconnecting door. The safety glass shattered but held firm and Barker tumbled through in a forward roll movement, twisting in mid-air and ending at the far end of the adjoining carriage facing inwards. The gun was already raised and pointed.

"Stay where you are," he ordered.

Peters was not quite so lucky. As he conventionally followed through behind, the bulk of Wainwright grabbed his arm and propelled him horizontally along the floor where he collided with the detective. The effect was enough for Gary to lose his balance and his gun, which clattered to the floor.

There was a pent-up rage in the pockmarked face of Wainwright as he stood towering over the two grounded men.

"I should have finished you while I had the chance Barker," he roared.

Gary extricated himself from under the policeman's body.

"Like you did Stephano," he taunted "and Mitchell?."

"Stephano was a greedy little runt who wanted more but Mitchell – I didn't do in Mitchell. You!" he commanded to the Inspector who was now seated legs apart on the carriage floor. "You keep still whilst Mr Barker here makes a play for his gun."

The gloating, sunken eyes bore into Gary. The man was past the point of reasoning and he knew as Wainwright stood there, his right hand in sheepskin coated pocket, that it's fingers were curled around a gun of some description. He was not imagining that tell tale bulge.

"Better make the play Barker," said Wainwright "I'm going to kill you anyway. You've caused me to much trouble, what with your snooping at my depot and at the warehouse."

"Don't be a fool man," interjected Peters. "If you kill him, you'll have to kill me and the other police officers who'll be waiting at the next station."

Before Wainwright could answer, the train slewed into a tight bend on its single-track structure and there was a scurrying action from behind him. He turned slightly off balance to see Candy and the other man hastily retreating through the broken remains of the inter-connecting door.

"Candy ..... Dino," he shouted. "Wait I ....."

The slight pause was the moment Gary had been praying for. He hurled himself at the bigger man and thrust him back down the aisle of the carriage. All the Queensbury rules were now forgotten as he punched and kicked out at him. A left to the stomach had the Etherton man wheezing for breath and a sharp right crunched horribly into his nose. Wainwright reeled and staggered further backwards at an angle and his heavyweight frame shook the carriage as he listed drunkenly into its sliding doors.

The man was not beaten yet however. He reached into the jacket pocket and pulled out the gun. There was a loud 'crack' and a faint aroma of cordite drifted across the occupants' nostrils.

Wainwright clamped a hand over his bloodied wrist and glanced across at Peters who was stood in the gunfighter position holding Barker's Baretta.

The fight still refused to be knocked out of the man and he aimed a kick at the detective's ribs. Gary neatly sidestepped this and followed up with a pile-driving right hook to Wainwright's jaw. The body seemed to lift itself up by its boots and hang momentarily in mid-air before crashing against the train's doors, which inexplicably began sliding open.

There was a sound of a female screaming. "No Patrick no." Gary was nursing his pained wrist as a streak of black passed by him.

She was holding him, tugging at his body, tearing his clothes, as the big man found himself suspended half-in and half-out of the carriage.

Gary reached to grab hold of her as the train rocked precariously on the rails with its uneven weight distribution. Wainwright struggled with his fading strength to grip hold of the nearest thing at hand to scrabble to safety. A further scream pierced the night air. It was a sharp, child-like agonising wail of terror and again it was unmistakeably feminine.

The train slowed as it approached Connington Station. Peters handcuffed the two men whilst Barker covered him with the Baretta.

Absentmindedly, Gary opened the battered suitcase. At the top, covering wads of English banknotes was a set of red accountancy books with the words "Caledonian" emblazoned across in gold lettering.

"So this was what Herbert had died for!" he mused, as the chill night air filled the carriage through the gaping entrance of the now stationary train.

****

She wasn't dead when they reached her but Gary knew it was only a matter of time. The elongated fall from the monorail system onto the tarmac below left little hope.

She was lucid and apparently in little pain – probably as much as a result of the shock as her shattered spinal chord.

She wanted to talk and Gary wanted to listen. They hadn't moved her. It seemed sensible not to. From her position, as the jigsaw puzzle began to fit, it seemed ironic that directly above her the monorail still functioned, taking the few remaining Connington Towers customers back to the car park terminus.

"Herbert," Gary said gently. "What's it been all about?"

"Greed," came the whispered response. "Greed and the love of a man." She hesitated, gathering her life blood's strength.

"You probably know that the Compton Arms was used as a staging post in MID-EX UK's operations. Dino Rossi not only controlled the UK element of a multi-national import/export agency on a legitimate basis but together we operated a profitable sideline trafficking in whatever the black market would take. We've sold pornographic material and drugs to the UK market and arms to Middle East concerns or whoever else required them. We have various 'dead-letter' drops all over England and business was growing all the time."

"You used beer barrels to move your stuff?" Gary prompted.

"Yes. It had worked so well before. Customs never checked. Things began to go wrong due to a simple mistake, which I made. It was becoming increasingly difficult to me to live three lives. I set up Patrick Wainwright as Transport Organiser for this area. He's a big bear as far as men are concerned but a baby when it comes to women. He thought I was his girl but I was playing with his emotions – leading him on – that sort of thing. He didn't know I was in love with Dino Rossi or that I planned to leave Jeremy when the final shipment was over. Even so, I liked him. He was like a father to me; one I never had."

The words were beginning to come a little harder now. Gary shone a torch into her face. As the tears began to flow he noticed the colour in her cheeks was draining rapidly. He was full of compassion, wanted to help but realised there was little he could do. He gently wiped the fluid away with a handkerchief.

"I went to see Mr Stephano at the Compton Arms. He'd been getting greedy, demanding more money for storing goods. He threatened to blow the gaffe. I was carrying the books, which Dino asked me to look after concerning our operations. Inadvertently I picked up the wrong set of accounts when I left the pub and it wasn't until I got back to my boutique that I realised I had the pub's accountancy books by mistake.

It was late by the time I returned and I saw Herbert Mitchell's Toyota there. I remembered that Jeremy had said something to me about the Stephano's being new clients and I knew that if Mr Stephano gave him the books I had left, then the whole operation would be finished. I didn't know what to do. I telephoned Dino. He was furious and told me to get the books back at any cost.

I couldn't very well go in and replace them – not with Herbert there. He was a very shrewd and clever man, although I've never really got to know him personally.

I decided to wait in the back of his car. It was midnight when he left with the books. He got into the car and studied them. I had no option, it was obvious he realised they were not the pub's books!

I forced him to drive to my brother's house. I knew it was unlikely anyone would find him there as he's away in Saudi Arabia. I drugged him with chloroform, connected the hose, switched the books and left the engine running. I wanted to make it look like suicide."

"So you didn't cut his throat?" asked Gary

"No – no – it was to be suicide. I – I couldn't kill in that manner!"

"I believe you," said Gary. He was convinced she was telling the truth, it was unlikely she would lie in a dying confession. But if Candy Roberts hadn't killed him, who had?

As Gary had suspected, the ambulance arrived too late to save her- not that there was much they could have done. She went peacefully, her head cradled in his arms and at the moment of departure from this earth, he doubted that such a lady had died looking quite so beautiful!

Chapter Seventeen

"So what your saying Gary is that Wainwright used his transport operation to shift beer barrels around the country to pick-up or drop-off illegal merchandise and he did it under the instruction of Candy Roberts who in turn answered to Dino Rossi. It all sounds a little far fetched to me!"

"The clever crimes often do," said Gary. "Using the brewery's own transport was too risky but there's still the question of Herbert Mitchell's death. Who do you think was responsible?"

"Couldn't it still have been Miss Roberts?"

Gary didn't think so. He believed the woman's dying confession. She had no reason to lie.

The Rover was making good progress along the M5 heading back for Etherton and both men were considering the events of the evening.

Inspector Peters was relieved that his impulsive action in pursuing two criminal suspects had been justified but he was aware that there was still an opportunity for a double success, providing Sgt Grainer had acted according to orders concerning the nightclub. The clock on the car dashboard showed ten past nine and there was ample time yet to organise a raid.

Gary sat alongside him hardly noticing the miles slipping away. He knew he was not as fit as he should be and that once he got back to Main City he promised himself he would grab hold of his partner Jason to organise a training programme for the two of them. Certainly they both needed it!

Mentally he was going over the facts. He understood why Wainwright had beaten-up Stephano. The man was besotted by Candy Roberts and would stand for no nonsense from anybody trying to put pressure on her for more money. Wainwright was the type who punched first and asked questions later. Could he have followed Candy and Herbert to 'Peaceful Waters' and killed Mitchell after she'd left. But what would be the point of that – Candy had already set up his death through carbon monoxide poisoning. So if it wasn't him - who did that leave? It wasn't Rossi because he was in London that evening as per Candy's information concerning the telephone call. That really only left the Stephanos' themselves, Jeremiah Cowling or Mitchell's partner Roberts.

Cowling did have a motive – albeit a slim one. He'd not been happy with the way Mitchell and Roberts had handled his accountancy affairs. Would he arrange a murder for a 'cock-up'? Gary thought that much as he disliked the man, it was unlikely he would do such a thing over something so trivial. Roberts too he dismissed. The smoothy 'yuppie' had an alibi substantiated by several people who were at a mediaeval banquet near Tewkesbury.

So as Mr Stephano was now deceased, perhaps he should concentrate his efforts on Maria. He remembered how she'd reacted when he'd asked her whether Herbert had been involved with Mr Stephano and the storage of merchandise in the pub's cellar. Her speech had been indignant at such a suggestion but the look in her fiery eyes had hinted at something more – a secret perhaps?

"Inspector," he questioned formally. "Where did Maria Stephano say she was on the night of Mr Mitchell's murder?"

"Before or after he left?"

"After"

"If I remember she said she went to bed at around quarter to twelve – migraine I think. What are you driving at?"

"Did she have a separate sleeping arrangement from her husband?"

"Why yes. That's not unusual in the pub trade though. Someone has to get up early to bottle-up, see to the beer pipes – that sort of thing."

"Does the bedroom overlook the car park?"

"Well eh yes."

"I think Inspector we should make a call to the Compton Arms first don't you?"

Peters looked across at the detective. What was the damn man thinking about. Surely the nightclub was the priority now.

As if reading his thoughts, the younger man responded.

"We'll still have time for the nightclub. What I have in mind shouldn't take long. If you're not careful you'll miss our motorway exit."

The policeman returned his eyes to the road ahead and pulled sharply left on the wheel as the headlights panned across the blue and white motorway sign indicating immediate exit for the A435 to Etherton.

As they left the motorway, Peters was forced to hit the brakes. For the last six hours they'd experienced the luxury of clear and fine weather. Now though, as the Rover dropped down into the Vale of Etherton – the menacing prospect of further fog threatened to envelop the English countryside.

Under his breath, Inspector Peters cursed. the speedometer dropped like a stone from 70 to 30 and the car's incumbents strained their eyes towards the windscreen and the grey blanket beyond.

Chapter Eighteen

"Are you alright?" asked Jacky showing considerable concern as Gary and Inspector Peters entered the public bar of the Compton Arms.

"Fine – a little bruised but all in one piece. Any chance of a drink?"

"Your boyfriend nearly damned well killed me," interjected Peters.

"The night's still young Inspector," laughed Gary. "What will you have?"

"If your buying it ought to be champagne but I'll settle for a pint of Brennards lager."

It was past closing time and the pub had a strange feel about it with the only lights showing being those over the bar. The expanse of space left vacant around the dart and pool table area, somehow gave it a spiritual air as if the regulars from past centuries had now taken it over for the nightclub shift till dawn.

Gary shivered, partly from the change in atmosphere but primarily from the lower temperature, which the night's fog had brought.

He looked at Jacky resplendent in a white Brennards tee-shirt pulled tightly over her full breasts. Two black palm prints – a little on the small side for her figure – did not completely cover the swellings. Underneath were the words 'Hands off – they're booby trapped'. Her jet-black hair had been 'frizzed' into a perm and Gary thought she wouldn't look out of place on one of those Hair magazine covers, which seemed to be everywhere these days.

"Like your hair," he said as she poured a beer. "Plugged it into a power point have you?"

She playfully swatted at him with a nearby towel used for wiping glasses clean but missed and caught the Inspector across his face.

"Oh I'm really sorry," she said and giggled uncontrollably. Peters took it in good stead and said

"I didn't know you cared." He picked up the fallen cloth and handed it back.

"Where's Mrs Stephano?" he asked.

Jacky's expression changed to one of concern.

"She's upstairs. I'm really quite surprised by the way she's come through this. Paul and I being novices at this game could not have managed without her. She put on a brave face for the punters and it's been quite an evening. I've had several offers you know," she said knowingly to Gary.

Gary was having difficulty tearing his eyes away from her chest. The outline of her lacy bra was clearly evident.

"I can believe it," he said. "Where is Paul?"

"Cleaning up in the lounge. Did you catch Wainwright and Roberts?"

Gary looked across at Peters who nodded his approval.

"Yes – we got them. But unfortunately *she* didn't make it."

"Oh. What happened?"

"Tried to save Wainwright's skin and ended up with a broken back. We'll talk about it later. Right now the Inspector and I need to talk with Mrs Stephano."

As if on cue the lady in question appeared through the pub's kitchen adjacent to the bar. She looked composed and was conservatively dressed in a simple black dress as a mark of respect to her dead husband. Her sultry eyes locked straight in on Gary's, which made him feel somewhat uncomfortable given the circumstances.

"It's over – isn't it?" she said simply.

"We have to ask you some questions," Gary replied lamely.

"Of course. Perhaps you'd like to bring your drinks through to the lounge?"

She walked with dignity, grace and with a certain poise and the two men followed as if hypnotised.

She sat there calmly awaiting the questions, her black stockinged legs showing just the right amount of thigh to gain the males' attention. Her gypsy hair, perfectly groomed, danced off her shoulders and the gold layers of jewellery glistened under the lounge lights.

Paul Mitchell re-appeared to join the group. The lanky youth acknowledged the mood of his elders and gently placed a glass of gin and a bottle of tonic beside her, before withdrawing and seating himself to one side.

Gary flitted his eyes from Maria to Paul and back again. The lady bowed her head, looked up at Gary and nodded. By this the detective thought that whatever she had to say would not upset the young man too much.

As no one appeared to want to open the conversation, Gary took the initiative.

"I understand your bedroom overlooks the pub's car park," he said.

"And on the night Mr Mitchell visited the pub in his professional capacity, you were in that bedroom?" he prompted.

"Yes"

"Did you happen by any chance to look out into the car park to where he'd parked his car?"

Maria now said nothing.

"You did didn't you – and you saw someone in that car – another woman?"

"What are you getting at Barker?" interrupted Inspector Peters.

"Please Inspector – it's all right. I want to answer. I realise now is the time."

Maria's words were quietly spoken with a serene quality. It was however, a voice racked with emotion caused by having to bear a considerable weight on one's conscience for too long.

"Yes Mr Barker. I did see a woman. A woman who was dressed all in black – a very beautiful woman with blonde hair. She was sat in the rear of Herbert's Toyota sports car."

Gary could almost feel the jealousy in her voice. He noted

to that it was the first time she'd referred to him by his Christian name.

"I didn't understand," she continued. "We'd been so discreet in our relationship. We weren't harming anyone and I thought we had an understanding. There was a little spark missing in both our marriages and it was exciting for us both to meet pre-arranged and without commitment. Our affair was purely physical passion to compensate for our respective partners sexual familiarity within marriage. It wasn't love or anything like that, we just had a need for one another. Herbert was a sweet man and I didn't think he could hurt me by falling for another woman or that he'd even consider someone else. Even when I saw Mrs Roberts in the car I had my doubts. What was she doing in the rear?" Why not wait in the passenger seat?

It was because I knew she was a flighty lady that the doubts grew stronger. She was so pretty you see – all the men fell for her!"

She paused and looked at both Gary and the Inspector as if looking for an agreement to this piece of information.

"I grew more suspicious when Herbert crossed the car park and got into the car. The floodlight overlooking the car park deceived me. I couldn't see what was really going on. It looked as though she was leaning forward and kissing his neck.

I followed in my car. They travelled down a country lane on the outskirts of Etherton and turned into a driveway of a place called 'Peaceful Waters'. I didn't know what to do. Everything seemed so unreal, I couldn't believe what was happening. I parked my car in some bushes and travelled on foot to the house. By the time I arrived she was coming out of a garage. I stood and watched. She pulled down the garage door and ran towards me. She passed by so close to me that I could even smell the perfume that she was wearing. Then all was still. Nothing happened. I waited and waited but still there was no sign of Herbert.

I was anxious by now. Before, it looked as though the two of them had come to this house as illicit lovers. Now I wasn't sure what to think. I tentatively approached the garage doors and reached for the handle. What happened next was confusion. It was dark, I couldn't see ..... The door swung up and these fumes swept out almost choking me. I stepped back and out of the blackness a shadow loomed menacingly. It appeared through the fumes and smoke. I thought I was trying to protect myself as I swung my arm up to fend off this grotesque attacker. There was a horrible gurgling sound. It was horrible – like the sound of water disappearing down a plughole. It seemed to go on and on. The figure before me was staggering like a drunk and trying to say something but the words couldn't get out. His hands reached out for me. They clawed at my shoulders, my breasts, my hips and finally my legs. After what seemed an eternity the body collapsed to the gravel.

I was in tears and frightened. I still didn't understand what was going on. I lit a match to see what it was that had attacked me. It was Herbert's face lying on its side that greeted me and from his neck pumped the blood. I could feel something sticky on my hand. it was his blood. I'd thrown up my arm to protect myself and the jagged stone in my ring had raked across his neck. I realised at once I'd accidentally killed him but who would believe me?"

She turned to Paul. Gary could tell the adolescent was trying hard to contain himself but he was man enough to realise that Maria was telling the truth.

"I'm sorry Paul – truly I'm sorry." She hesitantly held out her hand to him for some comfort and he took it and clasped it between his own."

"The bewilderment and look of astonishment in his eyes as he lay there I shall never forget and I realise the guilt must live with me for the rest of my life. I don't know what happened afterwards – I just ran as fast as I could."

Maria's head dropped and her free hand came up to her brow.

"I think the statement can wait until morning Mrs Stephano," said the Inspector. "Perhaps eh – Miss eh – Jacky you wouldn't mind staying with her for a while."

"It's all right," Paul interrupted "I'll stay."

Peters nodded.

"Right then lad. Barker and I have some unfinished business to attend to at Justine's nightclub. You coming too Miss?" he asked raising his eyebrows quizzically to Jacky."

"Yes – yes of course."

The two of them left the lounge whilst Gary lingered in the doorway.

He looked back at Maria and Paul consoling one another. The lad had lost a father, the woman a lover. She'd lost him through another woman's greed and her jealousy. He'd lost him through a frightful accident by the woman he was consoling. It was touching, yet terribly sad. He hoped that once the legal formalities were out of the way that such feelings for one another would remain mutual.

Gary wondered whether Paul would have the strength to help both his mother Joyce and Maria the landlady through the traumatic periods ahead. Only time would tell but at least he was making a brave start.

"Herbert," Gary thought, "Would have been proud of him!"

Chapter Nineteen

Jeremiah Cowling was livid. As he paced up and down his office, the light from the overhead candelabra picked out the glistening droplets of perspiration on his bald head. Nervously he dabbed at his head with a handkerchief.

"For Christ's sake Almond," he said, "this whole operation is falling apart at the seams and all you can suggest is that we sit it out. Remember son – you're in it to, right down to your size ten feet. If as you say – Detective Sgt Grainger has this nightclub under surveillance with other officers, I look to you to get me out. As it is now, we're sitting ducks!"

The young black officer stood calmly before the two-way mirror looking down at the disco-dancing below. Now that the pubs had closed the place was filling up rapidly with Ethertons teenage fraternity. The blue laser streaks bounced rhythmically to the 'rapping' sounds supplied by Justine's resident disc jockey and this turned the club into a 'Star Wars' style spectacular.

He turned round and faced the short man who in his eyes was now visibly squirming before him. Even the hard edge in Cowling's voice had disappeared. The man was pacing up and down like a crazed animal.

PC Almond had not been the top black recruit at Hendon for nothing. He had a shrewd and clever brain. From being in a position of taking 'backhanders' from Cowling for turning a blind eye to his criminal activities in the field of pornographic movies, he now realised the tables had turned! In his mind's eyes, he was in an excellent position to exploit this by returning to his lawful role.

"Relax Mr Cowling," he said. "Grainger won't make a move without the Inspector's authority. Very much a 'by the book' man is Sgt Grainger. We don't want to precipitate events by leaving the premises and forcing him to detain us, thereby exposing ourselves to a premature raid and seizure of your films. So I suggest you run the nightclub as per usual and kick the punters out at 2pm. I will then divert the officers at the rear of the building round to the front and you can make good your escape."

"I don't like it," said Cowling. "If your trying to double-cross me, you'll live to regret it I assure you."

The officer smiled laconically. He was unconcerned by this half-hearted attempt at a threat. Whatever happened now, Almond realised he was forced to act the part of the upright decent British bobby. Since Sgt Grainger had ordered him back into the nightclub – the odds had changed. It was now too dangerous to continue as a 'bent' copper!

The black and gold telephone receiver rang on Cowling's desk and he eagerly grabbed it. Seconds later Cowling slammed it down.

"Wainwright's been picked up," he said, his voice showing further alarm. "The plan's changed – there's no time to lose. Get Bert!"

"What are you going to do?"

"Just do it!"

Almond turned and made to move slowly towards the door. As he did so he noticed Cowling heading for the rear door of his office. He knew that the man would be clearing out his safe and that if that was the case, his own position was in jeopardy. If he remained in the office with Cowling, the man would as like as not kill h im. After all – if Wainwright was gone – his police services would no longer be required.

The constable's hand hovered over the handle of the main office door entrance. He was about to press the button on the police walkie-talkie on his uniform lapel, when the door was pressed ignominiously into his face.

"Don't let him leave Bert," barked a voice from behind him and he didn't need to look to see that Cowling had pre-empted his move. He also knew by the tone of voice that Cowling had him covered.

"So what happens now?" the officer asked lamely.

"We could hold you hostage but I can't be sure that Wainwright didn't talk to the police. It may be well known that you're a bad risk. So given the circumstances I intend to bluff my way out of this by using your uniform."

"You can't be serious man. For one thing your far too short"

Cowling reached into his desk draw and extracted a pair of scissors.

"It's dark out there and anyway you're still going to make that transmission which you were attempting to make just now. Only your call for assistance will be that I am making an escape at the rear of the club which means I will be able to walk out the front with little or no police activity."

"You're crazy," said Almond. "You'll never get away with it."

"I think you are in no position to judge"

The bottom lip of Cowling's Roman jaw line curled downwards into a sneer. The waiting game was over. Now that the action was pending, inner strength had returned and no longer did the overhead light identify beads of perspiration. Now, there weren't any!!

Chapter Twenty

"Shall we go in sir?"

Inspector Peters looked at his watch.

"What do you think Gary?" he asked, turning to the detective.

The three men stood waiting in the shadows opposite the nightclub. The fog had lifted slightly but it was still a chilly and gloomy November night.

"When do they close the club Sergeant?" he asked.

Sgt Grainger clapped his hands together back and forth trying to get some circulation into his fingertips. He'd been staking-out the club since early afternoon and now wanted to get home to his wife and kids. He was grateful of course for the Inspector's trust in letting him set up the operation but the thought of more waiting was just too frustrating to consider.

"2 o'clock sir but they'll be some early drunks out soon. No doubt they'll be pissing in the shop doorways, kicking car headlights and fighting amongst 'emselves as usual!"

"On the other hand," said Gary noticing the older man's discomfort "if we go in now Sgt we could lose that little weasel Cowling in the panic created by a police raid."

"Point taken," said Grainger. He was about to add his feelings concerning the facts that whilst the two of them had had an exciting day, his had been monotonous – when PC Almond's voice cackled through on his two way R/T.

"Cowling's made a move sir – round the back. PC Almond's calling for assistance."

"Almond?" interrupted Gary. "Tall – sly-looking black constable?"

"Yeah that's him!"

"I'd hedge my bets on that officer. Could be a trap!"

Peters thought for a second. He'd discussed the young officer with Sgt Denny at the station on a number of occasions. Though the man apparently disappeared on occasions, his trustworthiness and loyalty to the police force had never been questioned. On the other hand, Barker was a good judge of character - he was not to be ignored!

"How did he sound Sgt?" he asked.

"Edgy," came the blunt response.

"Take three men with you Les – we'll cover the front. Keep in radio contact with me here."

"In the meantime Dougie, I'm going in," said Gary.

The Inspector said nothing. He knew it would be pointless to argue with him. When Barker had a mind to do something, the Pope himself couldn't change it. Not that the man was Catholic of course"

"Hang-on. I'm coming too!"

Gary spun round in the small, cobble-stoned courtyard that fronted Justine's nightclub. The pair of replica coachman-style lamps above the entrance door cast a narrow red beam through the mist as Jacky approached him.

"I thought I told you to wait in the car," he said.

"What – and let you have all the fun in a nightclub. Oh no – too many feminine temptations in there," she chided. "Besides I've done too much hanging around for you in the last couple of days, I'm beginning to think I'm a hooker!"

Gary was distracted by a group of revellers as they left Justine's. He wasn't sure but they seemed too tightly packed together as if trying to conceal something or more to the point someone!

"Cowling," he stated in a loud but cool manner.

The youths turned and boisterously made drunken gestures.

"Hey man – what's your problem," one said "stick with your woman. Don't give us a hard time"

The pack however still appeared too close together.

"What's wrong love!" he heard Jacky say and then he caught a glimpse of a shiny baldhead,

Without regard for personal safety he dived into the group. The collision with half a dozen drunks had them scattering together with their bottles of beer in all directions. All that is – except for the man in what appeared to be a tattered police uniform.

Cowling was up and running fast. Gary made as if to follow but a deep gravelly voice made him stand firm in his tracks.

"You ain't going nowhere Mister Barker – cause if you do – your pretty gal here will be gathering lilacs amongst the clouds!"

The drunken youths, all of a sudden, were nowhere to be seen – swallowed up in the November mist.

Cowling's 'heavy' – the man called Bert had his left arm around Jacky's neck in the crux of his elbow. His right arm held the largest revolver Gary had ever seen. He couldn't be sure in the limited light available but it looked suspiciously like a Magnum. The detective instantly recalled that ballistics had identified the bullet, which he'd extracted from the lamppost as coming from a Magnum. Inspector Peters had been quite explicit about that!

"Bosses order," boomed the heavy, his arm tightening around Jacky's neck. "You upset him on your visit asking questions about the accountant Mitchell. Told me to scare you off the trail. One has to remain loyal to the boss you know!"

"So what happens now?" said Gary shrugging his shoulders and gesturing with his hands that he was unarmed.

"First you gently remove the hardware from inside your jacket and place it on the ground. Then me and your girlfriend will take a little trip in the car – after I've killed you of course!"

The man removed the Magnum from Jacky's head and pointed it at the detective.

"The gun Mister Barker!" he ordered.

There was the sound of shattered glass piercing the still air and momentarily the Magnum swung away from Gary's chest towards the cobblestones. A pained expression crossed Bert's face before his gun arm recoiled from the impact of a bullet fired from the private investigator's Baretta. It all happened so fast that the protagonists appeared caught in a time vacuum.

As the smoke faded, Gary could be found with an arm around Jacky's shoulders and a foot on the collapsed body of Cowling's 'heavy'.

"Thanks Paul," he said. "I owe you one"

"It was your gesture towards one of those empty beer bottles that did it. Mrs Stephano wanted to be left alone so I decided to come here. I have to confess I really enjoyed belting that large ape. He was always picking on Eddie and me in the nightclub. I reckon it was him that mowed him down with his car in the hit-and-run!"

"I think you're probably right son," said Gary as he ruffled the young lad's hair with his free hand.

Inspector Peters approached from the main road pushing the handcuffed Cowling before him. Seeing Barker with his foot on Bert's body and the Baretta in his hand he said approvingly

"Barker. You and I are getting better. Just like the Mounties – we always get our man!"

"He's your man now Inspector," came the response. "Come on you two," he said to Paul and Jacky. "The club's still open let's go and celebrate. I rather fancy a champagne disco!"

Chapter Twenty-One

"So how's life in the sticks?" Jason Lear hardly glanced at his senior partner as he entered the cramped offices of GB Private Investigations.

A flying newspaper clipped the ear of the dashing younger detective.

"Here – read about it in the Etherton Journal and take your feet off the desk – you uncivilised cannibal."

Gary strode across the office to his desk by the window where he stood and looked out over Main City. It was good to be back.

"Any messages?" he asked.

"On your desk. Heh – looks like you've stirred things up down there. According to this paper, you cracked a murder, solved a case of illegal trafficking of drugs, arms and pornographic films, weeded out a bent copper and scored the winning goal in a charity football match. What's it feel like to be a celebrity?"

"This celebrity is glad to be back doing real detective work. Here Jason bank this, will you!"

"Phew," he said. Real detective work doesn't pay as well as this you know!"

"Yes," said Gary. "Mrs Mitchell was very generous. I think she was relieved to discover that her ex-husbands professional reputation was not sullied."

He eased himself into his battered office chair and reached for the top piece of paper in his 'IN' tray. It was a bill for the accident in the SAAB. It appeared the fault in steering was not the manufacturers' responsibility and could they have settlement by return of post!

Gary bunged the bill over in the form of a paper aeroplane to his partner.

"Just enough in that cheque to settle my car," he said. "Now then – any meaty detective work outstanding? How about something juicy like a rape, blackmail, even espionage?"

Jason gave a boyish laugh.

"Got one here right up your street," he said. "How about a little debt collection?"

The End

Printed in the United States
1546600006B/28